U.A.P.

UNEXPLAINED ANOMOLOUS PHENOMENA

Mason Zabian

Mason Zabian
COPYRIGHT 2024

INFYNITY
MEDIA & PUBLISHING
LONDON, ONTARIO, CANADA
DEVERON CRESCENT
PEOPLEPOWER9991@YAHOO.COM
Available in all book formats
EBOOK, AUDIOBOOK,
PAPERBACK, HARDCOVER
https://www.facebook.com/profile.php?id=61567248003566

Copyright © 2024 Mason Zabian
All rights reserved.

Table of Contents

DEDICATION .... Error! Bookmark not defined.

Foreword: vii

The Unfolding Mystery of UAPs vii

Chapter 1: ix

Chapter 2: xv

Chapter 3: xxii

Chapter 4: xxix

Chapter 5: xxxvi

    Chapter 6: xliii

    Breaking the Silence: Interviews with Whistleblowers xliii

    Chapter 7: l

    The Scientific Debate: What is Really in the Sky? l

    Chapter 8: lvii

    UFO Technology: Secrets of Advanced Craft lvii

    Chapter 9: lxiv

    Encountering the Unknown: Personal Accounts lxiv

    Chapter 10: lxxi

    A Global Government Conspiracy? lxxi

Chapter 11: lxxix

    The Race to Control Space lxxix

    Chapter 12: lxxxvi

    The Future of Humanity and UAPs lxxxvi

    Chapter 13: xciii

    The Unseen Forces Behind UAPs xciii

    Chapter 14: c

    The Choice c

    Chapter 15: cvii

    The Unseen is Always There cvii

Conclusion:..cx
The Aftermath of Truth..cx
Case Files and Reports..cxvi
Resources for Further Reading...cxviii

DEDICATION

✧ ✦ ✧

To my cherished Grandparents and Parents, whose love, guidance, and sacrifices have been the foundation of my life.

To my Grandparents, who took me in on Dufferin Avenue and surrounded me with the warmth of their home and their hearts. I am forever grateful for the love, strength, and values they instilled in me. They didn't just raise me—they shaped me, imparting wisdom and resilience that have guided me through every chapter of my life.

I hold a deep admiration for them, having watched them work tirelessly as they built a new life in Canada, overcoming challenges with courage and grace. As immigrants, they left behind the familiar to give us, their family, a life filled with possibilities, a good home, and an abundance of love. I am in awe of their journey, their resilience, and their boundless generosity.

They taught me the importance of family, hard work, and staying true to one's roots, no matter where life may take us. Though they are no longer by my side, their presence lives on in every word of this book, and I feel their love guiding me each day. I miss them terribly, and I look forward to the day when I will see them again.

To my Parents, for their support and encouragement and for passing down the legacy of love that has been the bedrock of our family—I am eternally grateful.

Thank you for believing in me, for your unwavering support, and for showing me what it means to be loved.

Foreword:

The Unfolding Mystery of UAPs

For centuries, humanity has looked to the stars with curiosity, wonder, and perhaps a bit of fear. We've charted the heavens, sent probes to distant planets, and yet one question remains stubbornly unanswered: **Are we alone in the universe?**

In recent years, the phenomenon of Unidentified Aerial Phenomena (UAPs) has captured the public's imagination like never before. What was once relegated to the fringes of conspiracy theories and science fiction has now found its way into serious conversations, government investigations, and mainstream media reports. No longer are UAPs dismissed as the stuff of fantasy. They are real, they are here, and the world is finally starting to take notice.

This book seeks to illuminate one of the most perplexing mysteries of our time: the undeniable presence of UAPs, their potential origins, and the global efforts to understand them. Drawing on a wealth of declassified documents, firsthand testimonies from military personnel, and the latest scientific research, this book presents a case that demands our attention. Whether UAPs are manifestations of advanced human technology, the work of otherworldly intelligences, or something even more mysterious, their implications for our future cannot be overstated.

For decades, governments around the world have kept tight control over UAP-related information. The veil of secrecy is slowly being lifted, but even now, the full truth remains elusive. In the following pages, you will find a collection of **case files, reports, and witness testimonies** that challenge conventional explanations and suggest that we are on the brink of a profound discovery.

More than just a catalog of encounters, this book invites readers to think critically about what UAPs mean for humanity. Are they visitors from another world, products of interdimensional travel, or perhaps evidence of time manipulation? As we delve deeper into the UAP phenomenon, we are forced to confront fundamental questions about our place in the universe and our understanding of reality.

The following chapters will take you through key incidents, from the well-known military encounters to lesser-known but equally compelling civilian reports. We will explore the **scientific, political, and cultural dimensions** of UAPs, as well as the deep ethical and philosophical dilemmas they pose. Should we fear what we do not understand, or should we embrace it as the next step in our evolution?

This book doesn't claim to have all the answers, but it does present evidence that demands further investigation. The truth is out there—perhaps closer than we ever imagined.

As you turn these pages, I invite you to keep an open mind. The phenomenon of UAPs challenges our assumptions and forces us to think beyond the limits of our current knowledge. Whatever the final answers may be, one thing is certain: the **unseen** is always there, and it is waiting for us to explore it.

Chapter 1:

The Awakening of Mr. Rockerfeller

The hum of the city faded into the distance as **Mr. Rockerfeller** stared out of his Manhattan apartment window. It was a typical summer evening in New York City, hot and thick with humidity, but something felt different tonight. He couldn't shake the unease that had settled deep in his chest.

The world outside bustled, but Mr. Rockerfeller's thoughts were elsewhere. A banker by trade, but a lifelong seeker of truth, he had spent years quietly fascinated by mysteries that the world overlooked. Like many others, he had heard about the occasional UFO sightings, those flickering reports on late-night radio shows or obscure corners of the internet. He always dismissed them, content to believe the common explanation: weather balloons, experimental aircraft, tricks of light. But tonight, something tugged at him. Perhaps it was the steady uptick in UAP reports making headlines over the past few months. Every day it seemed, another story emerged: unidentified craft appearing over major cities, captured on military radars, spotted by commercial pilots. The world's governments, once dismissive, had become notably silent.

He poured himself a glass of water, trying to ease the tension he couldn't explain. As he sipped, something caught his eye—a glimmer of light high in the sky, just above the skyline.

It started as a faint, blinking star. But then it moved.

At first, he thought it was a plane. Yet the object wasn't behaving like any aircraft he'd ever seen. It darted across the sky with an eerie smoothness, its movements sharp and sudden, unlike the steady pace of any plane or helicopter. It blinked out of existence for a moment, and then reappeared, much closer than before.

Mr. Rockerfeller set the glass down, his heart now racing. The object hovered over the rooftops, close enough that he could see it wasn't any traditional aircraft—it was a metallic disc, featureless except for a faint glow at its edges. He fumbled for his phone, trying to capture a video, but as soon as he raised the camera, the object shot upward into the sky with blinding speed, disappearing into the blackness of space.

His phone slipped from his hand, clattering onto the wooden floor.

The room suddenly felt too small, too claustrophobic. His pulse quickened as a thousand questions flooded his mind. He had just witnessed something—something extraordinary, something that couldn't be explained by the rational world he knew. His instinct told him to call someone, to report it, but to whom? What would he say?

In the stillness of his apartment, it dawned on him: This was just the beginning.

The next morning, the usual grind of the city did little to calm his mind. The sighting haunted him, playing on a loop every time he blinked, every time he glanced up at the clear blue sky. He couldn't just let it go.

Mr. Rockerfeller took a different route to work, deciding to walk through the park instead of taking the crowded subway. His feet crunched over the gravel path, his mind replaying the previous night's events again and again. As he walked, he spotted a group of men gathered around a public bench, huddled closely, talking in hushed voices.

One of them was holding a newspaper. The headline screamed out from the page: "**Mysterious Object Spotted Over New York Skies: Military and FAA Refuse to Comment**."

His heart skipped a beat.

He made his way over, casually pretending to stretch by a tree as he eavesdropped on their conversation.

"You see it, too?" one man asked the others. He was older, wearing a baseball cap pulled low over his eyes.

"Yeah," said another, a younger man with a heavy New York accent. "Right over the East River. Lasted about a minute, then zipped outta there. Military ain't sayin' nothin'. No surprise there."

The third man, a nervous-looking fellow, chimed in. "I swear, it's like they don't even care. Just like all those other sightings they're covering up. You see what's going on over in Europe? Same thing. Lights over Paris two days ago. Nothing. No explanation."

Mr. Rockerfeller's stomach knotted. The pattern was undeniable now. This wasn't an isolated event. It was happening all over the world. He couldn't shake the feeling that what he'd seen was connected to something much bigger—something that the public wasn't being told.

That night, sleep was impossible. Mr. Rockerfeller sat at his desk, his laptop screen glowing in the dim light of his study. He started researching, his fingers moving fast across the keyboard. At first, it was innocent enough: local news websites, UFO forums, archived government documents. But the more he dug, the darker the rabbit hole became.

He found declassified files from the Pentagon—reports of encounters with unidentified flying objects that military pilots had chased but could never catch. He stumbled upon an old documentary that detailed secret government projects like **Project Blue Book**, meant to investigate UFO sightings during the Cold War. The deeper he went, the more he realized how little the public actually knew, and how much governments around the world were deliberately keeping hidden.

Each new discovery felt like a small shock to his system, building an overwhelming sense of dread. Could it really be that there was a massive cover-up happening? Was humanity in contact with something beyond Earth—and if so, why were world powers working so hard to suppress it?

Then, just past midnight, his inbox dinged.

The email address was unfamiliar, but the subject line made his pulse spike: "**For Your Eyes Only: Read Before They Find Out**."

He clicked it open, his hands trembling.

The email contained a single link, no message. He hesitated, hovering over it, the cursor blinking. Every part of his rational mind told him to stop, that he was being paranoid. But something else, something deeper, pushed him to click.

The screen flickered and then a grainy video appeared. The footage was shaky, clearly shot on a handheld camera. It was a nighttime shot, deep in a forest somewhere. Mr. Rockerfeller watched as the camera panned upward. Hovering in the sky above the trees was a glowing orb, far too large and far too silent to be any known aircraft. The video zoomed in closer, capturing the object in remarkable detail. It had the same eerie glow he had seen over his apartment just hours earlier.

Then, there was a voice, a hurried whisper from the person filming. "They don't want us to know. They're coming…"

The screen went black.

For a long moment, Mr. Rockerfeller sat motionless, staring at the darkened screen. He felt a chill creep down his spine. This wasn't just a coincidence. Whoever had sent him the video knew something. But who were they? And why had they reached out to him?

Suddenly, his phone buzzed beside him. It was a text from an unknown number.

"**Stop digging, Rockerfeller. Or you won't like what you find.**"

His blood ran cold.

Someone was watching. Someone knew what he was doing, and they wanted him to stop. But he couldn't—not now. Whatever this was, it was far bigger than him, far bigger than the governments who were hiding it. The world needed to know the truth, and he was going to find it, no matter the cost.

Should we modify or extend this chapter, or shall we move on to the next chapter?

Chapter 2:

The Global Surge: Sightings Across Continents

The weight of that cryptic message sat heavy on Mr. Rockerfeller's shoulders. He spent the following days looking over his shoulder, questioning every stranger who made eye contact with him a second too long. The world had taken on a sharper, more dangerous hue, but something else also changed: a relentless hunger for the truth. He couldn't stop now, not when the pieces of this vast puzzle were starting to come together. What he had seen over the New York skyline wasn't an isolated incident—it was part of something much bigger, and it wasn't just happening in his corner of the world.

The more he read, the clearer it became: these sightings were global.

It started in Europe. From news clips to conspiracy blogs, sightings had surged across the continent. Reports of strange lights above the Pyrenees, erratic movements of objects over Germany's Black Forest, and silent, metallic orbs floating above the Eiffel Tower flooded in. Civilians, military personnel, and even commercial pilots started breaking their silence. What was once the stuff of whispers and secret UFO clubs had now burst into the public consciousness.

One case in particular caught Rockerfeller's attention: **the Paris Incident**.

It happened just two weeks before he'd seen the object in New York. On a late summer evening, tourists and locals strolling along the banks of the Seine spotted an unexplainable light in the sky. What began as a single, bright object quickly multiplied—four lights forming a perfect diamond shape above the city. Videos posted to social media went viral within minutes. Eyewitnesses described the lights as moving with unnatural speed and precision, faster than any known aircraft could manage. They darted in formations, weaving around one another like they were performing some kind of otherworldly dance.

Rockerfeller watched video after video, each more compelling than the last. The craft didn't make a sound, not even the faint hum of a helicopter or jet engine. Then, after nearly twenty minutes of hovering and weaving above Paris, they disappeared in a sudden flash, leaving nothing behind except a city full of stunned witnesses.

French military authorities claimed they had no record of any aerial activity in that airspace. When pushed by the media, they offered little more than vague explanations about "atmospheric anomalies" or "optical illusions." But the people who were there knew better. Something had visited Paris that night—something not from this world.

From Paris, Mr. Rockerfeller's investigation led him to **Chile**, a country with a long history of UFO sightings, especially in the remote northern desert regions. The Atacama Desert, one of the driest places on Earth, had long been a hotspot for unexplained phenomena. Local villagers had told stories of strange lights appearing in the skies for decades, but in recent months, the activity had increased dramatically.

He reached out to **Dr. Elena Ramirez**, a Chilean scientist and renowned UFO researcher, who had dedicated her life to studying these occurrences. She was cautious at first, wary of another curious civilian diving into a field that had already seen its fair share of skeptics. But as he shared his own experiences and began exchanging the data he'd uncovered, she opened up.

Over a late-night video call, Dr. Ramirez explained the situation in Chile.

"It's not just sightings anymore," she said, her face grim on the flickering screen. "We've recorded physical traces—radiation spikes, electromagnetic disturbances. After one sighting, entire power grids went offline for hours. We've even found burns in the ground where these craft have supposedly landed."

She shared a file of pictures with him: circles scorched into the desert floor, each about 15 meters in diameter. The burns were impossibly precise, as though they had been made by some sort of intense heat, yet no fire or explosion had been reported. She mentioned cases where local farmers had reported seeing small, humanoid figures near the landing sites, always vanishing into the desert before anyone could get too close.

"These aren't just lights in the sky anymore," Dr. Ramirez continued, her voice lower now, as if someone might be listening. "Whatever they are, they've started interacting with our world in ways we can't explain."

Her words haunted him. For the first time, Rockerfeller began to consider the terrifying possibility that these UAPs weren't just passive observers—they might have a more active role in the world than anyone wanted to admit.

From the deserts of Chile, his research turned to **Russia**, where sightings were becoming increasingly hard for the government to cover up. Russia had long been a nation obsessed with control, and the Kremlin was no stranger to rumors of hidden extraterrestrial research programs dating back to the Cold War. The famous **Tunguska event** of 1908, where a massive explosion flattened thousands of square miles of forest, was often linked to UFO folklore. Official reports claimed a comet or meteor, but whispers of alien involvement never completely died down.

Now, in 2024, sightings were on the rise again.

Siberia, in particular, had become a hotbed of UFO activity. In a small, isolated village outside Yakutsk, locals reported a massive cylindrical object hovering silently above their town for hours. It emitted a low, resonant hum that locals could feel in their bones, rattling windows and setting off car alarms. Unlike in Paris or Chile, where the objects quickly vanished, this one stayed—floating in place as if watching, observing.

One witness, a retired Russian Air Force officer, managed to capture a high-resolution photograph of the craft. The image was stunning: a sleek, metallic cylinder with no visible engines or wings. There were no markings, no signs of human design. After 45 minutes, the object rose vertically into the clouds and disappeared. Local authorities were quick to arrive, confiscating the officer's camera and silencing the village with threats of military detention.

Yet somehow, a copy of the photo made its way to the internet before being scrubbed from most websites. It was already spreading like wildfire in conspiracy forums by the time Rockerfeller found it.

There it was again— the same eerie glow around the edges of the craft, the same impossible smoothness that made it feel less like an object and more like a phenomenon.

Rockerfeller couldn't shake the thought: these weren't isolated events. They were connected, part of a larger pattern.

A week later, Rockerfeller was knee-deep in his research when an email pinged his inbox. This time, it wasn't anonymous. The sender was **Carlos Alvarez**, a former Chilean air force pilot turned independent investigator. He had seen the Atacama reports and wanted to share his own findings with Rockerfeller.

Alvarez wasn't just any pilot—he had been part of an elite squadron tasked with intercepting unidentified aircraft near Chilean airspace. "We were never supposed to talk about it," Alvarez wrote. "But I've had enough of the lies. People deserve to know."

The retired pilot described a routine patrol flight he had taken in 2023. Flying over the Pacific Ocean, just off Chile's coast, his radar picked up something unusual—a fast-moving object closing in from above. But when he looked up from his instruments, there was nothing in the sky. The radar, however, showed the object moving directly towards his plane at impossible speeds.

Before he could react, his jet shook violently. A flash of light blinded him, and suddenly, the object appeared directly in front of his cockpit—a silver orb, featureless and silent. It hovered there for what felt like minutes but was likely only seconds. Then, as quickly as it had come, it vanished, leaving his jet systems fried. He barely managed to glide back to the base.

"I know what I saw," Alvarez wrote. "And it wasn't human."

The deeper Rockerfeller dug, the more he realized that this wasn't a new phenomenon. For decades, UAPs had been crisscrossing the globe, their presence increasing in frequency and boldness. From **Japan** to **Australia**, from the **Brazilian Amazon** to the **Swiss Alps**, sightings were happening everywhere.

There were reports of UAPs disrupting military exercises, causing electrical disturbances in civilian cities, and even sightings near nuclear power plants. The world's governments were struggling to maintain control over the narrative as more and more evidence leaked out, but each time the truth got too close, something always stepped in to shut it down.

It wasn't just the United States that was involved in the cover-up. It was global. Nations that could hardly cooperate politically were somehow united in their efforts to silence any real investigation into UAPs. The question wasn't just *what* these objects were anymore. The real question was: **why were the world's powers so desperate to hide them?**

As Mr. Rockerfeller closed his laptop late one night, his eyes red from hours of research, he couldn't help but feel that the answer was closer than ever before. But the closer he got, the more dangerous this journey became.

He poured himself a cup of coffee, staring out the window again at the city below. His mind raced with possibilities, his paranoia growing. Someone was watching him, and they knew he was getting too close. But now that he had started unraveling the thread, there was no going back.

The world was watching, too. And it was only a matter of time before the truth came crashing down.

Shall we modify or extend this chapter, or shall we move on to the next chapter?

Chapter 3:

Governments in the Shadows

The sharp ring of the doorbell jolted Mr. Rockerfeller from his thoughts. It was late—too late for visitors. He glanced at the clock: 11:45 p.m. His heart thudded in his chest, anxiety spiking. He hadn't told anyone about his research, not even his closest friends, but lately, the feeling of being watched had grown stronger. The text message warning him to stop digging echoed in his mind.

He approached the door cautiously, peering through the peephole. A deliveryman stood outside, a package in his hands, his uniform soaked from the drizzle outside. That was strange. Rockerfeller hadn't ordered anything. Slowly, he opened the door.

"Package for Mr. Rockerfeller," the man said in a monotone voice. His eyes were tired, and he didn't seem particularly interested in small talk.

Rockerfeller signed the form and took the box, closing the door quickly behind him. He set the package on the kitchen table, staring at it. There was no return address, only his name and apartment number scrawled in black ink on a plain brown cardboard box.

A sinking feeling settled in his stomach. He tore it open, pulling out a thick manila envelope. Inside, there were files—declassified government documents, each stamped with the insignia of a different country. The United States, Russia, the

United Kingdom, China. And at the very bottom, a small USB drive taped to a handwritten note.

"This will explain everything. Be careful who you trust."

His hands trembled as he reached for the USB drive. He hesitated for a moment, the enormity of this mystery weighing down on him, before finally plugging it into his laptop. The screen blinked as the drive auto-loaded. A single folder appeared, titled "**Dark Sky Initiative**."

The files inside were staggering.

The first document was a briefing paper, apparently written by a high-ranking official within the **United States Air Force**, dating back to 1974. It detailed an international covert operation tasked with investigating and controlling information about UFO sightings. The initiative, codenamed **Dark Sky**, wasn't just about studying UAPs—it was about **containing the truth**. It coordinated efforts between the world's leading governments to manage public perception, suppress information, and, if necessary, discredit or silence witnesses.

Rockerfeller's breath caught in his throat. This wasn't just a local conspiracy. This was global, deeply entrenched within the world's most powerful nations, and it had been going on for decades.

For hours, he combed through the documents. The more he read, the clearer the picture became: Dark Sky wasn't just about keeping UAPs secret. It was about

control—control over information, over the narrative, and ultimately over **technology** that could change the balance of global power.

The next file outlined an international summit held in **Geneva in 1991**, where high-level officials from the **U.S.**, **Russia**, **China**, and **several European nations** met in secrecy to discuss the growing number of UAP encounters. The meeting minutes were chilling. Governments around the world were not only aware of UAPs—they were **studying them**, and in some cases, attempting to **reverse-engineer** the technology.

But something in the documents stood out. There were references to an organization that wasn't part of any government—something larger, more secretive. A network of powerful individuals from various sectors: military, intelligence, finance, and technology. The documents referred to them only as the "**Cabal.**" The name was always accompanied by vague mentions of "discreet funding" and "covert operations," but the details were elusive.

Suddenly, it all made sense. These governments weren't just suppressing the truth—they were protecting their **interests**. The Cabal had its hands in everything, ensuring that no nation would unilaterally benefit from the technology that these UAPs might hold.

As the hours wore on, Rockerfeller's growing sense of unease deepened. He scrolled through pages of reports detailing UAP incidents that had never made it into the public domain: military pilots vanishing after chasing strange objects, entire villages in remote regions of the world wiped off the map with no explanation, satellite images showing craft hovering above nuclear facilities.

Then he found the video.

It was buried deep in a folder titled **"Top Secret: Incident Recordings"**. The timestamp read **July 2008**. The video was grainy, seemingly taken from a helicopter, flying low over a dense jungle. The footage showed a massive, dark metallic craft slowly descending into a clearing. Soldiers, dozens of them, wearing uniforms without insignia, were waiting below. They surrounded the craft, some carrying equipment while others aimed their weapons at the ship as if expecting a threat.

There was no sound, just the eerie silence of the jungle and the ship. For nearly three minutes, the soldiers held their positions, the craft suspended in mid-air. And then, without warning, it disappeared. One moment it was there, the next it was gone—no flash, no sound, nothing. The soldiers stood motionless, their heads scanning the sky.

The video cut off abruptly.

There was a file attached to the video labeled **"Operation Black Lotus: Encounter Debrief"**. Rockerfeller opened it, eyes scanning the text, his heart pounding. The report confirmed that the incident took place in the **Congo Basin**, one of the most remote and inaccessible regions on the planet. It also detailed the aftermath: the entire squadron involved in the operation was later found dead, their bodies showing signs of radiation exposure, though there had been no detonation of any weapon.

The conclusion of the report was stark: "**The craft demonstrated capabilities far beyond any known technology. Their ability to appear and disappear raises concerns about dimensional or temporal manipulation. Recommend continued investigation, but extreme caution advised.**"

Rockerfeller leaned back in his chair, staring at the screen. His mind was spinning. Governments were aware of these crafts—hell, they had been interacting with them. But the implications were even more disturbing than he had imagined. If these crafts were capable of **dimensional** or **temporal** manipulation, the possibilities were terrifying. The ability to move through time or across dimensions would give whoever possessed that technology **ultimate power**.

This was why the Cabal existed. It wasn't just about keeping UAPs a secret from the public—it was about controlling a technology that could reshape the world.

The following days were a blur of paranoia and relentless research. Rockerfeller found himself diving deeper into the Dark Sky Initiative, tracing its roots through decades of political agreements, covert funding schemes, and military black-ops operations that spanned continents. The web of secrecy was vast and complex, involving high-ranking officials, tech moguls, and even religious leaders.

But the more he uncovered, the more dangerous it became. His phone calls started to drop. Emails went unanswered. One night, while walking home from a late meeting with a contact, he noticed a black SUV following him through the city streets. He turned down an alleyway, heart racing, only for the vehicle to pass by without slowing. Still, the message was clear: **they were watching him.**

Then came the final straw. One evening, as he was sifting through yet another trove of documents, his laptop screen went black. For a split second, he thought it had crashed, but then a single message appeared:

"You've gone too far, Mr. Rockerfeller. This is your last warning."

The screen blinked back to life, and the files he had been combing through were gone—erased without a trace.

His heart raced. He was now certain that he was in over his head. Dark Sky was real, and the Cabal was working relentlessly to ensure that their control over UAP technology remained undisputed. The message was clear: if he continued, there would be consequences. But Rockerfeller knew there was no turning back. He had seen too much, learned too much. The world deserved to know what was going on—about the encounters, the cover-ups, and the terrifying truth behind these crafts.

He stood at the window of his apartment, staring out at the city, the skyline lit up like a sea of stars. Somewhere out there, above the clouds, something was watching. And down here, in the shadows, the Cabal was watching him.

Rockerfeller knew one thing: the deeper he went, the more dangerous it became. But he also knew that the only way to truly understand the phenomenon was to keep digging, no matter the cost.

Shall we modify or extend this chapter, or shall we move on to the next chapter?

Chapter 4:

The Media Cover-Up: Silencing the Truth

The newsroom buzzed with the kind of controlled chaos that signaled something big was happening. Reporters huddled around their desks, whispering into phones or tapping away at their keyboards, while televisions mounted on the walls streamed breaking news. But none of the headlines had anything to do with what Mr. Rockerfeller knew was unfolding behind the scenes. The world was being bombarded with distractions: political scandals, celebrity mishaps, and economic forecasts—anything to keep attention away from the rapidly escalating number of UAP sightings.

Rockerfeller stood in the middle of it all, feeling invisible. He had managed to arrange a meeting with **Lisa Monroe**, one of the top investigative journalists for the nation's largest network. Her stories on government corruption and corporate greed had won her multiple awards, and she was known for her dogged pursuit of the truth. If anyone could break this story wide open, it was her.

But as he watched her glide from one conversation to another, he realized how difficult it was going to be. The media wasn't just ignoring the UAP issue—it was **actively suppressing it**.

Monroe finally spotted him and motioned for him to follow her to a corner conference room, away from prying eyes. As soon as the door closed, she turned to him with a wary smile. "You've got fifteen minutes. Make it count."

Rockerfeller wasted no time. He pulled out the manila envelope he had been carrying since his encounter with the Dark Sky documents and spread the contents across the table. Monroe's eyes scanned the papers—official reports, photos of UAPs, references to the Cabal—but her expression remained impassive.

He had expected shock, or at least interest. Instead, she sighed and leaned back in her chair. "You're not the first person to bring me something like this, you know."

Rockerfeller blinked. "You've seen these documents before?"

"I've seen **pieces** of them," she said, her tone resigned. "And I've tried to get them out. But the thing is, there are layers to this—deep ones. You publish one story about UAPs, maybe even get some traction, but it doesn't last. The powers that be come in, and suddenly your story is buried. Editors tell you to back off, sources dry up, and before you know it, the whole thing just… disappears."

She paused, then lowered her voice. "There's a reason why UFOs don't make front-page news, Mr. Rockerfeller. And it's not because people aren't interested. It's because someone, somewhere, **doesn't want us talking about it**."

Monroe's words hit him harder than he expected. He had suspected a media cover-up, but to hear it confirmed from someone on the inside was different. He had naively thought that once he found the right journalist, the story would spread like wildfire. But now, the reality set in: the media was complicit, either willingly or unwillingly, in keeping the truth about UAPs hidden.

He leaned forward. "But why? Why would they want to suppress something so monumental? The public has a right to know."

Monroe glanced around, as if checking for invisible ears listening in. "Look, I don't have all the answers. What I do know is that the media is controlled by larger forces than just networks and advertisers. Governments, corporations—they have a stake in this. If the truth about UAPs came out, it could destabilize everything: the economy, military power, even religion. And whoever controls the narrative controls the world."

Rockerfeller felt a chill creep down his spine. "So what do we do? How do we break through?"

Monroe sighed again, her hands running through her short, dark hair. "You keep trying. You find cracks in the system. Small outlets, independent journalists, people who aren't afraid to lose their jobs over this. But even then, it's a long shot."

She stood up, gathering the papers. "I'll look into this, but I can't make any promises. The higher-ups—" she hesitated, her eyes darkening, "—they have their orders, and they don't mess around."

As she walked him to the door, Rockerfeller couldn't shake the feeling that she had already resigned herself to the story never seeing the light of day.

After the meeting, Rockerfeller's frustration mounted. The media blackout wasn't just about protecting secrets—it was about **controlling the public's reality**. But why now? Why the sudden increase in UAP sightings, and why were the governments of the world so invested in keeping this knowledge hidden?

He decided to broaden his scope, digging into past cases of media suppression. The further he went, the clearer the pattern became. This wasn't a new phenomenon.

In the 1940s and '50s, **Project Blue Book**, the U.S. Air Force's public investigation into UFOs, had been designed as much to discredit UFO sightings as it was to investigate them. For years, officials had downplayed sightings, labeled witnesses as unreliable, and buried reports that couldn't be easily explained. The media played along, framing the UFO phenomenon as fringe science, the domain of conspiracy theorists and crackpots.

But behind the scenes, governments were treating the matter with deadly seriousness. The files from **the 1967 Malmstrom Air Force Base incident**—where witnesses reported UAPs disabling nuclear missile systems—had been **classified for decades**. And when the story finally did leak, it was spun as an unverified, exaggerated account. Anyone who tried to take the story seriously was met with skepticism, even ridicule.

Rockerfeller kept reading. There were countless other examples. The **Phoenix Lights** in 1997, where thousands of witnesses saw massive, silent craft moving over the city, was dismissed by the media as a flare drop by the military. The **Nimitz Encounter** in 2004, where U.S. Navy pilots had engaged with UAPs that defied the laws of physics, had only recently been acknowledged after years of official denial—and even then, the full details were kept under wraps.

Even in the digital age, where information flowed freely, the powers that be had found ways to **control the narrative**. Social media platforms, once a bastion of free speech, were increasingly subject to influence. Algorithms buried UAP content, fact-checkers labeled witness accounts as "unsubstantiated," and the few outlets brave enough to report on these stories were drowned out by more mundane news.

One night, Rockerfeller received a message from an anonymous source claiming to work at a major news network. The message was simple but chilling:

"We have standing orders from higher-ups to avoid UAP stories. Anything that gets too much traction is killed. They're watching. Don't push too hard."

Who **they** were remained a mystery, but Rockerfeller had his suspicions. The Cabal, the same shadowy group pulling the strings behind the Dark Sky Initiative, clearly had its hands in the media, too. The scope of their influence seemed limitless.

As the days passed, the frustration grew unbearable. Rockerfeller started reaching out to smaller, independent news outlets, desperate to find anyone willing to report on the files he had uncovered. But even there, the responses were hesitant. Some journalists expressed interest, but when they followed up with their editors, the stories were quietly dropped. A few reporters even stopped returning his calls altogether.

One night, while sitting in his darkened apartment, Rockerfeller's phone rang. The voice on the other end was low, cautious.

"Mr. Rockerfeller, this is **Mark Young**. I'm a producer for a small independent podcast that covers conspiracies and government cover-ups. I heard you're looking for someone to run your story."

For the first time in weeks, Rockerfeller felt a flicker of hope.

They met a few days later at a quiet coffee shop in the East Village. Young was a wiry man in his early thirties with an unshaven face and a restless energy about him. As they sat down, Young leaned in, his voice barely above a whisper. "I've been trying to get something like this out for years, but every time I get close, I hit a wall. My last attempt—about a CIA mind-control experiment—got me blacklisted from most networks. But this UAP stuff? This is on another level."

He paused, his eyes scanning the room nervously. "You understand the risk, right? If we go public with this, we're going to piss off a lot of powerful people."

Rockerfeller nodded. He had come too far to turn back now.

Young smirked, leaning back in his chair. "Good. Because once we push this out there, there's no going back."

The next few weeks were a whirlwind of secret meetings, encrypted emails, and late-night editing sessions. Together, they compiled a bombshell podcast series, detailing everything from the Paris Incident to Dark Sky to the Cabal's influence over the media. Rockerfeller's files served as the backbone of the investigation, and Young's storytelling flair brought the story to life in a way that was both gripping and chilling.

As they neared the release date, the tension was palpable. They both knew that once the series went live, there would be consequences.

Finally, after weeks of preparation, the first episode of the podcast, titled **"The Silent Sky"**, dropped.

Within hours, it was spreading like wildfire across conspiracy forums and social media. Listeners were shocked by the depth of the cover-up, and as more people shared the episode

Chapter 5:

A Web of Secret Organizations

The first episode of **"The Silent Sky"** ignited a firestorm. Within days, the podcast had gone viral, racking up thousands of downloads and sparking heated debates across social media and alternative news platforms. The general public was finally starting to ask the right questions, but with that came an inevitable pushback. Powerful forces had taken notice, and it didn't take long for Mr. Rockerfeller to feel the full weight of their retaliation.

Anonymous threats flooded his inbox. "Shut it down, or you won't make it to next week," one message warned. His phone rang late at night—silent calls from unknown numbers. Shadows seemed to follow him everywhere he went. One evening, after returning home from another meeting with Mark Young, Rockerfeller found his front door slightly ajar. Inside, nothing appeared to have been taken, but someone had rifled through his files, his laptop left open on his desk with a single document flashing on the screen: **"STOP."**

He was being watched, and they were no longer bothering to hide it.

Meanwhile, **Mark Young** had gone dark. He'd missed several calls, and then one morning, Rockerfeller received a cryptic message from an encrypted number:

"Too dangerous. They're closing in. Keep pushing forward. You're on your own now."

Rockerfeller's hands shook as he stared at the message. Young had been fearless, eager to uncover the truth no matter the risk. For him to suddenly vanish meant that whatever they were dealing with was far more dangerous than either of them had anticipated.

In the days following the release of the podcast, Rockerfeller dug deeper into the labyrinth of secret organizations that seemed to be operating behind the scenes. The name "**The Cabal**" appeared over and over in the files he had recovered, always in reference to meetings, covert operations, or funding initiatives, but the exact nature of this group remained elusive.

He pieced together fragments of information—whispers from old contacts, scattered references in declassified documents, and obscure mentions in conspiracy forums. What emerged was a chilling picture: The Cabal was a shadowy network of global elites—an alliance of military generals, government officials, corporate titans, and intelligence agents from across the world. Their goal wasn't just to suppress knowledge about UAPs; it was to **control** the technologies that came with them.

From the Pentagon to Moscow, from Silicon Valley to the European tech sectors, The Cabal's reach extended into the highest echelons of power. They had been operating in the shadows for decades, coordinating secret missions to recover UAPs and studying their technology. Governments, military forces, and tech companies were just pawns in a much larger game, and The Cabal sat at the top, pulling the strings.

The Origins of The Cabal

Rockerfeller traced The Cabal's origins back to the aftermath of **World War II**. In the early days of the Cold War, UAP sightings became more frequent, particularly near military installations and nuclear testing sites. These craft, capable of defying gravity and traveling at unimaginable speeds, posed a new kind of threat—one that couldn't be met with conventional weaponry.

Governments around the world, particularly the U.S. and the Soviet Union, were desperate to figure out the source of these crafts. Secret programs were launched to capture and reverse-engineer UAP technology. It was during this period, Rockerfeller discovered, that The Cabal was born.

Leaders from the world's superpowers realized that if they could harness the power of these advanced crafts, they would hold an insurmountable advantage over their enemies. But this technology was so far beyond anything humanity had ever seen that the risk of it falling into the wrong hands—or worse, becoming public knowledge—was too great. To keep control, the heads of these programs formed an alliance, agreeing to work together in secret, away from the prying eyes of their own governments and the public.

Over the decades, this alliance grew into The Cabal, with new members inducted from the world's most powerful sectors. What had started as a covert military operation had evolved into a global conspiracy with the sole purpose of controlling and suppressing information about UAPs.

The Black Budget Programs

One of the most disturbing revelations Rockerfeller uncovered was how The Cabal used **black budget programs**—secret projects funded by governments with no public oversight—to carry out their agenda. These programs were cloaked in layers of secrecy, hidden from even the most senior officials within the governments that funded them.

Through leaked documents, he discovered one such program: **Operation Nexus**, a joint initiative between the U.S. and European military intelligence agencies. Launched in the early 2000s, Nexus was tasked with recovering UAP debris from crash sites around the world. These were the remnants of craft that had malfunctioned or been downed by experimental military technology.

But the true purpose of Nexus was far more sinister. The project didn't just involve recovering debris—it also focused on abducting individuals who had witnessed UAP events or had come too close to the truth. These people were either "re-educated," discredited, or, in extreme cases, made to disappear entirely.

Rockerfeller felt a cold chill as he read these files. Governments were not only aware of UAPs, but they were actively **controlling** who knew about them and **silencing** those who posed a threat to their secrecy.

Deep Underground Bases and Secret Laboratories

As Rockerfeller pushed further into his research, another disturbing trend emerged: the existence of **underground bases** and **secret laboratories** where UAP technologies were being studied in secret. These facilities, scattered around the globe, operated outside the bounds of traditional oversight and were funded through black budget operations.

One such base, **Site-7**, was reportedly located deep beneath the **Ural Mountains** in Russia. It had been rumored for years in UFO circles but never confirmed—until now. Leaked Russian documents referred to Site-7 as a joint military-civilian research complex where recovered UAPs were stored and studied. Reports of strange energy readings, unexplained phenomena, and even **extraterrestrial biological specimens** being housed there were referenced in cryptic notes by high-ranking Russian military officials.

The U.S. had its own version: **Groom Lake**, better known as **Area 51**. While the public was familiar with the rumors surrounding Area 51, the documents Rockerfeller found suggested that the base was merely a cover for the real research happening elsewhere. One such place was **Raven Rock**, a massive underground military complex on the East Coast, where UAP technology was being studied in complete secrecy.

Rockerfeller's investigations revealed a shocking detail: many of these underground bases were not just military operations but were run with **corporate oversight**. Mega-corporations, including tech giants and aerospace companies, had contracts with military and intelligence agencies to study and possibly replicate UAP technology.

Corporate Collusion

Corporations were a key part of The Cabal's operations. Aerospace companies like **Lockheed Martin**, **Boeing**, and **Northrop Grumman** were all implicated in the development of experimental aircraft using UAP technology. But it wasn't just aerospace companies. Silicon Valley had its own players in the game.

Rockerfeller uncovered a damning link between **technological innovations** over the last twenty years—artificial intelligence, quantum computing, and energy advancements—and the secretive UAP research happening in these underground facilities. Companies like **Google**, **Tesla**, and **SpaceX** were all listed in confidential government contracts as having access to data collected from UAP incidents.

It was no coincidence that the rise of technology had accelerated at an unprecedented rate over the last few decades. The Cabal had been carefully releasing UAP-inspired breakthroughs into the public sector, but only in ways that would benefit them and maintain their control.

One particular project, codenamed **Project Prometheus**, was a joint effort between the U.S. Department of Defense and several tech companies to reverse-engineer the propulsion systems of UAPs. The goal was to develop a new form of energy—one that could revolutionize the world's energy infrastructure and eliminate reliance on fossil fuels. But instead of sharing this technology with the world, The Cabal was hoarding it, using it to consolidate their power.

A Dangerous Crossroad

The more Rockerfeller learned, the more isolated he became. He had stumbled upon a vast web of secrecy, one that connected governments, corporations, and secret societies in a conspiracy that stretched across continents and decades. The Cabal was not only suppressing the truth about UAPs—they were actively shaping the future of humanity, controlling the flow of information and technology in ways that served their agenda.

He knew he had to get this information out, but with Mark Young gone and every avenue of mainstream media blocked, the question remained: **How?**

As he prepared to meet with another contact, someone he hoped could help him, Rockerfeller felt the weight of the knowledge he carried. The deeper he went, the more dangerous the game became. The Cabal was closing in on him, but he couldn't stop now.

The truth was out there. And it was only a matter of time before the world would have to face it.

Chapter 6:

Breaking the Silence: Interviews with Whistleblowers

The weight of the knowledge Mr. Rockerfeller carried now felt suffocating. With every piece of evidence he uncovered, the forces against him grew stronger. Mark Young had vanished, the media was compromised, and The Cabal seemed to lurk behind every corner, controlling not only governments but the very fabric of society. But despite their best efforts, cracks were beginning to show. Some people were starting to talk.

Whistleblowers, once silenced by threats, intimidation, or worse, were reaching out to him. They wanted to tell their stories—stories that had been suppressed, erased from the public record, and buried under layers of secrecy. These weren't just random civilians or fringe conspiracy theorists. These were military personnel, scientists, and former government agents. They had been on the inside, and now they were willing to risk everything to expose the truth.

The First Contact

It was through a secure messaging app that Rockerfeller received the first message. The sender identified himself only as **"Jacob"**, claiming to be a former intelligence officer who had worked within a highly classified U.S. government program studying UAPs. After days of cautious exchanges, Rockerfeller finally managed to arrange a face-to-face meeting in a small diner on the outskirts of Washington, D.C.

Jacob arrived late, slipping into the booth opposite Rockerfeller without saying a word. His face was drawn and haggard, eyes darting nervously around the room. He was wearing a baseball cap and sunglasses, despite the dimly lit interior of the diner. After a few tense moments of silence, he leaned forward and spoke in a low, hushed tone.

"I've been following what you've been doing," Jacob said, his voice barely above a whisper. "You're closer to the truth than you think. But if you keep pushing, they'll come for you. Like they did for me."

Rockerfeller sat silently, waiting for Jacob to continue.

"I worked for a program… one of those black budget operations that don't officially exist. We weren't just investigating UAPs. We were **reverse-engineering them**—trying to figure out how they worked, what powered them. This wasn't just theoretical work, either. We had real craft—recovered from crash sites, some in perfect condition, others… not so much."

Jacob paused, taking a deep breath. His hands trembled slightly as he pulled out a small black notebook, sliding it across the table. "These are the names of others like me—people who worked on the inside and know the truth. Some of them won't talk, but a few… they might. But you have to be careful. Every one of these names is a potential target for The Cabal."

Rockerfeller flipped through the notebook. The names were written in a neat, tight script, alongside brief notes—job titles, locations, and, in some cases, ominous details like **"missing"** or **"deceased."** It was a grim list, but it was also a lead—a way to crack open the tightly controlled world of UAP secrecy.

The Scientist Who Saw Too Much

Jacob's notebook led Rockerfeller to his next contact, **Dr. Evelyn Strauss**, a physicist who had once worked for a top-secret research facility linked to the **Defense Advanced Research Projects Agency (DARPA)**. She had been involved in studying the propulsion systems of a UAP that had been recovered from the Pacific Ocean after an incident involving the U.S. Navy.

Dr. Strauss agreed to meet him in a quiet café in New Mexico, far from the scrutiny of government eyes. She arrived early, her tall, lean frame blending easily into the sparse crowd. There was a certain calmness to her demeanor, but her eyes, sharp and calculating, held years of secrets she had longed to share.

"We knew from the start it wasn't human," she said, diving into the conversation without preamble. "The material alone was unlike anything we've ever encountered. Stronger than any known metal, yet somehow flexible. The propulsion system—it didn't run on fuel as we understand it. It was something… else. We couldn't replicate it, but we tried."

She paused, her eyes glazing over as if reliving the events. "When I started asking too many questions, they removed me from the project. Sent me to a different department, far away from anything related to UAPs. It wasn't just that they didn't want us to understand. They wanted to control the technology and keep it from the public."

Rockerfeller leaned in, intrigued. "What about the others in your team? Did they push back?"

Strauss shook her head. "Most were too afraid. They'd seen what happened to whistleblowers before me. Some who had spoken up mysteriously disappeared—'accidents,' they called them. But we all knew. They were silenced."

The Military Insider

Next on Rockerfeller's list was **Captain Raymond Nichols**, a retired U.S. Air Force pilot who had been involved in a top-secret mission to intercept UAPs over the Pacific in 2018. His story was one that had been quietly buried by the government, classified as an "equipment malfunction." But Nichols had seen something that couldn't be explained by faulty radar systems.

Meeting in a remote cabin deep in the Colorado Rockies, Nichols recounted his harrowing experience.

"We were flying routine patrols when our radar lit up like a Christmas tree," Nichols said, his voice steady but laced with the tension of recalling that day. "We thought it was a glitch at first, but then we saw it—an object moving faster than anything I've ever seen. It wasn't just speed, though. This thing was **playing with us**—zig-zagging, stopping on a dime, then accelerating out of our range in the blink of an eye."

He paused, running a hand through his graying hair. "I've flown just about every aircraft the military has, but nothing moves like that. We tried to lock on to it with our targeting systems, but it was like it knew what we were doing. Every time we got close, it just vanished off the radar, only to reappear behind us."

Nichols leaned forward, his voice dropping to a near whisper. "When we returned to base, they debriefed us—hard. They made it clear: what we saw never happened. They wiped the radar data, threatened us with court martial if we ever spoke about it. It was clear—**they knew** what we had encountered. This wasn't our first run-in with these things, and it wouldn't be the last. But they were covering it up, pretending like it didn't exist."

The Disappearance of John Bailey

Not all of the names on Jacob's list were willing to talk. One, in particular, haunted Rockerfeller: **John Bailey**, a former CIA operative who had gone underground after an incident involving UAPs in the Middle East. Bailey had been stationed at a secretive military base in Saudi Arabia when a UAP was spotted hovering near one of the oil fields. The event, captured on military-grade cameras, showed the craft silently observing the site before disappearing at an impossible speed.

Rockerfeller tried for weeks to track Bailey down, but every lead turned cold. Former colleagues of Bailey spoke in hushed tones, often refusing to even acknowledge his existence. Then, just as Rockerfeller was beginning to lose hope, he received an email from an anonymous source.

"Bailey isn't missing. He's dead. The Cabal got to him. Be careful, Rockerfeller. You're next."

It was a stark reminder of the dangerous game he was playing. The Cabal was always watching, and they had no qualms about eliminating those who threatened to expose them.

A Growing Web of Voices

Despite the risks, Rockerfeller's list of contacts grew. More whistleblowers reached out, each with their own piece of the puzzle. Some had worked for the **National Security Agency (NSA)**, intercepting signals from deep space that couldn't be explained. Others were former engineers for private aerospace companies, tasked with developing technology based on UAP designs. They all told the same story: a global conspiracy to suppress the truth about UAPs, to hoard their technology, and to silence those who dared to ask too many questions.

Rockerfeller began compiling their testimonies, piecing together a timeline of UAP encounters and the systematic efforts to keep them hidden. The pattern was unmistakable: **Governments knew**, but they weren't just hiding these encounters out of fear of public panic. They were actively **profiting** from the technology, while keeping the world in the dark.

As Rockerfeller sat at his desk late one night, reviewing the mountain of evidence he had gathered, he realized the enormity of what he had uncovered. The truth was no longer just a collection of rumors and conspiracy theories. It was real. Tangible. And more dangerous than he had ever imagined.

But with each new contact, each new revelation, came a fresh wave of danger. The Cabal was growing impatient. Their warnings were becoming more direct, more threatening.

Rockerfeller knew he had to move fast. The world needed to know what was happening, but with the media blackout and whistleblowers disappearing, time was running out. If he didn't act soon, the truth might be lost forever—buried under layers of government secrecy, corporate greed, and the shadows of The Cabal.

Chapter 7:

The Scientific Debate: What is Really in the Sky?

As Mr. Rockerfeller continued to gather testimonies from whistleblowers, he realized he had enough information to expose the government cover-up of UAPs. But one critical element remained uncertain—**the science**. What were these objects? What were their origins? Were they advanced military technology, extraterrestrial crafts, or something else entirely?

To answer these questions, Rockerfeller sought out scientists, physicists, and engineers who had either worked on UAP research or had studied the phenomena independently. He hoped they could shed light on what was truly behind the sightings and whether humanity had the capacity to understand—or replicate—the technology being used.

This chapter of his investigation would force him to confront not just the mysteries in the sky, but the very limits of human knowledge.

Dr. Samuel Hartman: The Skeptic Turned Believer

Dr. **Samuel Hartman** was a respected theoretical physicist who had once dismissed UAPs as little more than optical illusions, human misinterpretations of natural phenomena, or hoaxes. He had publicly criticized UAP believers, calling them "irrational" and "scientifically illiterate." For years, he was a staunch skeptic, writing articles for major publications debunking UFO sightings and explaining them away as weather balloons, experimental aircraft, or celestial bodies.

But in 2022, something changed.

Rockerfeller met Hartman at his lab in **Princeton**, where the once-cynical scientist had become one of the leading voices in serious UAP research. As they sat down in his book-lined office, Hartman's demeanor was calm but intense, as if the weight of a great secret had settled on his shoulders.

"I never thought I'd be saying this," Hartman began, "but after years of studying the data—real, hard data—I can't explain what I've seen. And that scares me."

Hartman shared with Rockerfeller the results of his research. For the past two years, he had been part of a team analyzing radar, satellite, and infrared data from **the Nimitz and Roosevelt UAP encounters**—the now-famous incidents involving U.S. Navy pilots who tracked objects that moved at hypersonic speeds, executed impossible maneuvers, and displayed no visible propulsion systems.

"What we're seeing defies the laws of physics as we understand them," Hartman said, his voice low. "These objects aren't just fast. They're **beyond fast**. They accelerate from zero to thousands of miles per hour in an instant, stop on a dime, and change direction at right angles. That kind of maneuvering should tear any conventional craft apart. But these UAPs show no signs of stress—no heat signatures, no sonic booms. It's as if they're moving through a different medium."

Rockerfeller was intrigued. "Different medium? You mean like space?"

Hartman shook his head. "No, something else. It's possible they're manipulating **gravity** or **space-time** itself. We're talking about technology that could bend the fabric of reality, possibly tapping into dimensions we can't perceive. That's not just alien technology—it's beyond what we even imagined was **possible**."

Hartman had also analyzed footage of the UAPs captured in the **Atacama Desert**, in Chile, and noted something even more bizarre: some of the objects appeared to "flicker" in and out of existence, suggesting they could be phasing between dimensions. "It's like they're not entirely **here** in our physical reality," he said, shaking his head. "We don't have the tools to fully understand what we're dealing with."

The AI Engineer: Reverse-Engineering UAP Tech

Rockerfeller's next stop was **Silicon Valley**, where he met with **Dr. Priya Mehta**, an AI and robotics engineer who had been secretly working on government contracts tied to UAP research. Mehta was part of a team attempting to reverse-engineer what she called "non-terrestrial materials" recovered from UAP crash sites. What she revealed to Rockerfeller was shocking.

"We've been studying alloys and compounds that don't exist on Earth," Mehta said as she led him through her lab. "At least, not in any form we can currently manufacture. These materials are incredibly light, yet unbelievably strong. Some of them have molecular structures that we can't replicate. It's like they're built at the **atomic level** with precision we can't achieve."

Rockerfeller was taken aback. "Are you saying this is alien technology?"

Mehta hesitated. "It's… not from **here**. I can't say where it's from. But it's far beyond our capabilities. The most advanced labs in the world have tried to recreate these materials, and they've failed every time. What's more, these materials seem to have **energy properties** we don't fully understand. When subjected to certain frequencies, they resonate and produce energy—clean, almost limitless energy. If we could unlock the secret to how these crafts are powered, it would revolutionize everything—energy, transportation, even our understanding of physics."

But it wasn't just the materials. Mehta's team had also been working on decoding the **propulsion systems** of UAPs. What they discovered was mind-boggling. "These crafts don't use fuel in the traditional sense," she explained. "They seem to harness some kind of **field propulsion**, possibly anti-gravity, by manipulating the space around them. We believe they're generating localized gravity wells, essentially 'falling' through space rather than flying through it."

Dr. Li Wei: Quantum Entanglement and the UAP Connection

In **Beijing**, Rockerfeller connected with **Dr. Li Wei**, a leading quantum physicist who had been involved in China's secretive UAP research. Dr. Wei had been studying a strange phenomenon linked to UAP encounters: **quantum entanglement**.

"There's a theory," Dr. Wei began, "that UAPs are using quantum entanglement to communicate or even to move through space instantaneously. Quantum entanglement is a phenomenon where particles become linked, no matter the distance between them. When one particle changes, the other reacts instantly—faster than the speed of light. Einstein called it 'spooky action at a distance.'"

According to Dr. Wei, some UAPs displayed behaviors that suggested they could be using this quantum principle to **move through space** in ways that seemed impossible. "It's as if they can appear in one place and then vanish, only to reappear elsewhere—like they're not traveling in the traditional sense but are instead **instantaneously relocating**."

Rockerfeller was stunned. "Teleportation?"

Dr. Wei nodded slowly. "Not quite, but close. It's more like… phasing. They may be operating outside our normal three-dimensional space and moving through higher dimensions. We've detected quantum signatures during some UAP sightings that suggest they're using entanglement or quantum tunneling to bypass the constraints of space and time."

The Skeptics: Natural Phenomena or Human-Made?

Not all scientists agreed with these extraordinary theories. Rockerfeller made a point to speak with those in the academic community who still held to more traditional explanations for UAPs. **Dr. Helen Morrison**, an astrophysicist at **Cambridge University**, believed many UAP sightings could be attributed to **natural phenomena**—atmospheric disturbances, lightning, or even solar flares.

"There are still so many things we don't understand about our own planet," Morrison argued. "Ball lightning, plasma fields, electromagnetic disturbances—they can all create the illusion of fast-moving objects or lights in the sky. While I agree that some UAP reports are compelling, I think we need more data before jumping to conclusions about alien technology."

Others, like **Colonel Robert Davies**, a former engineer with the U.S. military, believed UAPs were **human-made**, perhaps advanced prototypes developed by foreign governments or even private corporations. "Just because we don't know what they are doesn't mean they're from outer space," he said dismissively. "We've had stealth aircraft and drones for decades that the public didn't know about. Who's to say these UAPs aren't just a next-gen version of that technology?"

But for every skeptic Rockerfeller interviewed, there were dozens of experts who admitted that the more they studied UAPs, the less they could explain.

The Growing Divide

As Rockerfeller delved deeper into the scientific debate, he found a growing divide within the scientific community. On one side were the skeptics, who insisted that UAPs had rational explanations grounded in human technology or natural phenomena. On the other were those who believed UAPs represented **something beyond human understanding**, possibly extraterrestrial or interdimensional.

The tension between these two camps had grown as more UAP encounters came to light. Governments were forced to acknowledge the phenomena, but the explanations remained elusive. Were these objects manifestations of **cloaked military technology**, or were they evidence of **advanced civilizations** watching—and perhaps even interacting with—Earth?

For Rockerfeller, the truth seemed to lie somewhere in between. The testimonies from whistleblowers, the declassified documents, and now the growing body of scientific research all pointed to one inescapable conclusion: humanity was standing on the edge of a revelation that could change everything. Whether these objects were terrestrial or extraterrestrial, one thing was clear—they were far beyond anything the public had ever imagined.

As Rockerfeller compiled his findings, the urgency of his mission became clearer. He wasn't just investigating a mystery—he was documenting the first steps toward understanding a new reality. But with every revelation, he knew the stakes were rising. The Cabal had gone to great lengths to control UAP technology, and they wouldn't let him expose the truth without a fight.

And time was running out.

Chapter 8:

UFO Technology: Secrets of Advanced Craft

Mr. Rockerfeller stared at the endless expanse of the night sky through his apartment window, contemplating the strange technological revelations he had uncovered. The deeper he went, the more he realized that the UAPs, while seemingly alien in origin, possessed technology that might offer solutions to some of humanity's most pressing problems—if it weren't being so closely guarded.

The scientific data he had gathered was clear: these crafts were using propulsion systems, materials, and energy sources that defied the conventional understanding of physics. From **quantum entanglement** to **anti-gravity fields**, every piece of UAP technology hinted at breakthroughs that could alter life on Earth forever. But how had these craft come into human possession, and why were governments and corporations working so hard to keep them hidden?

The answer lay in the **secrets of advanced craft**—secrets that had been carefully guarded by the world's most powerful institutions for decades.

A Dark History of Reverse Engineering

As Rockerfeller dove deeper into the shadowy world of UAP research, he began to piece together a timeline of humanity's attempts to reverse-engineer the technology from these mysterious craft. It began with the **Roswell Incident** in 1947, where a UAP reportedly crashed in the deserts of New Mexico. The U.S. government had quickly moved to secure the wreckage, declaring it a weather balloon to the public. But behind the scenes, scientists were already studying the debris, and it wasn't long before secretive military projects were launched to unlock its secrets.

According to documents Rockerfeller uncovered, the U.S. wasn't the only nation involved in these covert efforts. The **Soviet Union** had launched similar programs in the aftermath of World War II, using technology recovered from crash sites in **Siberia** and **Eastern Europe**. The race to decipher these advanced crafts became the real arms race, with each superpower scrambling to gain an advantage over the other.

Rockerfeller had heard rumors of a vast network of underground laboratories, funded by **black budget programs**, where recovered UAPs were housed. These facilities, located in some of the most remote regions of the world, were guarded by private security firms and were completely off-limits to the public. The goal was clear: **reverse-engineer the alien technology** and use it to develop advanced weapons, energy sources, and propulsion systems that would give the controlling nation or organization **unmatched power**.

But progress was slow. While the materials recovered from the UAPs were unlike anything humanity had ever seen, the technology was so advanced that even the brightest scientists struggled to understand how it worked. According to one insider Rockerfeller spoke with, attempts to replicate UAP propulsion systems had led to **numerous accidents**, including mysterious deaths of several prominent engineers and scientists.

Still, the world's most powerful governments and corporations were undeterred. The potential of these technologies was too great to ignore, and the stakes were too high to let the public in on what was happening.

The Science of Anti-Gravity and Field Propulsion

Among the most tantalizing technologies recovered from UAPs was their **propulsion systems**. Unlike any known form of human flight, UAPs seemed to glide effortlessly through the sky, free from the limitations of gravity or atmospheric drag. They could accelerate from a standstill to hypersonic speeds in a split second, change direction without slowing down, and even hover in place—all without producing the intense heat or sound that would be expected from conventional aircraft.

Through conversations with whistleblowers and scientists, Rockerfeller discovered that these craft seemed to operate using a form of **anti-gravity propulsion**. The theory was that UAPs generated a powerful **electromagnetic field** around them, allowing them to manipulate gravity and inertia. By creating localized gravitational fields, these craft could "fall" through space in any direction, effectively bypassing the constraints of conventional propulsion.

Dr. Priya Mehta, the AI and robotics engineer Rockerfeller had previously met, had explained it in more detail. "It's like they're creating a bubble around themselves where the laws of physics don't apply in the same way," she had said. "Within that bubble, they're not affected by gravity, inertia, or even air resistance.

That's why they can move in ways that seem impossible to us—they're bending the space around them."

The implications of such technology were staggering. If humanity could replicate this form of propulsion, it could lead to a revolution in **transportation**, **energy production**, and even **space travel**. Vehicles could travel at incredible speeds without consuming fuel, and space exploration could advance at an unprecedented rate. Yet, as Rockerfeller uncovered more and more, it became clear that this technology was being **suppressed** for fear of its potential to disrupt the current global order.

Energy Beyond Imagination: Zero-Point Energy

One of the most significant breakthroughs in UAP technology involved their energy systems. UAPs seemed to operate without any visible fuel source, yet they exhibited incredible power, performing maneuvers that would require enormous amounts of energy. Traditional scientists had no explanation for how these crafts could generate such power without consuming conventional fuels.

But in the files Rockerfeller uncovered, there was a recurring mention of something called **zero-point energy**—a theoretical energy source that could potentially provide limitless power by tapping into the quantum field.

Dr. Samuel Hartman, the physicist Rockerfeller had met earlier, had touched on this during their conversation. "Zero-point energy is the energy present in the vacuum of space itself," Hartman explained. "Even in the emptiest parts of the universe, there's still energy—an unimaginable amount of energy. Theoretically, if we could access and harness that energy, it would solve the world's energy crisis overnight."

According to the classified documents Rockerfeller had obtained, several governments and private research firms had been experimenting with zero-point energy for decades, using technology recovered from UAPs as the foundation for their work. The goal was to create a **zero-point energy generator**, a device capable of pulling energy from the quantum vacuum and providing virtually unlimited power.

But the technology wasn't without its dangers. The files detailed **catastrophic accidents** that had occurred during attempts to harness this energy—explosions, radiation leaks, and even the collapse of localized space-time fields. The risks were so great that some governments had abandoned the research entirely, deeming it too dangerous to continue. Yet, others persisted, convinced that the potential rewards outweighed the risks.

For Rockerfeller, this discovery was the most alarming. The idea that world governments were sitting on a technology that could end global reliance on fossil fuels, eliminate energy poverty, and reshape the economy was both thrilling and terrifying. If zero-point energy became widely available, it would render the global energy markets obsolete, triggering an economic collapse in oil-dependent nations and industries. It was no wonder that The Cabal, with its vested interests in maintaining the status quo, had worked so hard to keep this technology hidden.

Dimensional Travel and Time Manipulation

Perhaps the most outlandish—and yet most fascinating—theory that Rockerfeller encountered was the idea that UAPs weren't just manipulating space, but **time** itself. Some of the scientists and whistleblowers he spoke to believed that UAPs might be using a form of **dimensional travel**, allowing them to slip between different points in space and time with ease.

Dr. Li Wei, the Chinese quantum physicist, had hinted at this during their conversation. "The way these craft move—it's as if they're not bound by our three-dimensional reality," she had said. "They phase in and out of existence, almost like they're traveling through a fourth dimension. It's possible they're using quantum entanglement or some form of exotic matter to achieve this."

The more Rockerfeller dug into this theory, the more it seemed to explain some of the more bizarre UAP sightings—cases where objects had appeared out of nowhere, vanished into thin air, or seemed to travel distances that should have been impossible in the time given. Some reports even suggested that UAPs might be able to manipulate **time dilation**, slowing down or speeding up time within their localized fields.

If true, this meant that UAPs weren't just advanced aircraft—they were potentially **time machines**. The implications were staggering. If humanity could unlock the secrets of dimensional travel, it would open the door to **faster-than-light travel**, **interstellar exploration**, and even the manipulation of time itself.

Why Keep It a Secret?

With each new revelation, the question loomed larger: **Why were these technologies being kept secret?** The potential benefits were immeasurable. From clean energy to faster-than-light travel, UAP technology could usher in a new golden age for humanity. Yet, The Cabal and the governments involved in UAP research seemed determined to keep it all under wraps.

The answer, Rockerfeller realized, was simple: **control**. Whoever held the keys to these technologies held unimaginable power. Energy, transportation, military dominance—all of it could be revolutionized by what was locked away in the underground labs and research facilities. But to release these technologies to the public would mean giving up that control. It would destabilize the global economy, challenge the political structures that had stood for centuries, and potentially lead to chaos.

The Cabal, with its deep ties to both governments and corporations, had too much to lose. As long as they kept the public ignorant, they could continue to profit from the current system while secretly developing UAP technology for their own purposes.

The Next Step

Rockerfeller sat at his desk, staring at the mountain of evidence he had collected. He knew he had to act soon. The world was being denied a future where energy was free, where space travel was possible, and where humanity could break free of the limitations of the physical universe. But exposing The Cabal and its grip on these technologies was risky. If they had silenced whistleblowers and scientists before, they wouldn't hesitate to do the same to him. But the truth was too important. And time was running out.

Chapter 9:

Encountering the Unknown: Personal Accounts

In the months following the viral release of the podcast **"The Silent Sky,"** more and more people began to come forward, reaching out to Mr. Rockerfeller to share their stories of encounters with UAPs. Some were ordinary citizens who had witnessed strange lights in the sky. Others were military personnel who had been forced to remain silent for years, bound by national security laws and threats from higher-ups. The pattern was undeniable: these sightings were happening all over the world, from the most remote wilderness to the busiest cities, and people were starting to demand answers.

Rockerfeller carefully documented each account, knowing that these personal stories were the key to building public awareness. These were not just isolated incidents; they were pieces of a much larger puzzle. The truth about UAPs wasn't just being concealed by governments and corporations—it was hiding in plain sight, buried in the experiences of ordinary people.

The Fishermen in the Pacific

One of the most compelling accounts came from a group of fishermen off the coast of **Chile**, near the Pacific Rim. These men had spent their entire lives working the ocean, battling the elements in one of the world's most treacherous fishing grounds. They were practical, no-nonsense men—hardly the kind to believe in science fiction or outlandish tales.

But on a cloudless night in late 2023, everything changed for them.

Rockerfeller met with **Juan Morales**, the captain of the fishing boat, in a small coastal town just outside of **Valparaíso**. Morales was a man in his late fifties, his weathered face and calloused hands testament to years spent at sea. He spoke calmly, but there was a tension in his voice—a deep unease that surfaced whenever he spoke about that night.

"We were about fifty miles out," Morales began, his eyes fixed on the horizon as if reliving the experience. "It was quiet—too quiet. The sea was calm, the sky clear. Then, out of nowhere, this light appeared. It wasn't like anything I've ever seen before. It was… too bright, too perfect. At first, I thought it was another boat, maybe a ship in the distance. But it was in the sky, hovering. And then, it started moving."

Morales described how the light darted across the sky with impossible speed, zigzagging in patterns no aircraft could replicate. His crew, hardened men who had seen just about everything the ocean could throw at them, were terrified.

"It moved closer," Morales continued. "Hovering right above us. There was no sound—nothing. Just this eerie silence. We could see the outline of the object now. It was metallic, like a disc, and it glowed around the edges. My men were shouting, some of them praying. We thought it was the end."

Then, just as suddenly as it had appeared, the object shot off into the night sky, disappearing in a flash of light. The entire encounter had lasted no more than five minutes, but it had shaken Morales and his crew to their core.

"We didn't talk about it for a long time," Morales admitted. "Who would believe us? They'd say we were crazy, or drunk, or worse. But I know what we saw. It wasn't from this world."

The U.S. Navy Pilot: A Close Encounter Over the Pacific

While the fishermen's account was chilling, it wasn't the only one Rockerfeller received from the Pacific region. Just weeks after speaking with Morales, he was contacted by **Lieutenant Commander Jack Mitchell**, a retired U.S. Navy pilot who had had his own close encounter while flying over the **Pacific Ocean**.

Mitchell had been part of a routine training exercise in 2018 when his radar picked up an unidentified object moving at incredible speeds. He and his wingman, both flying F/A-18 Super Hornets, were ordered to investigate. What they encountered would later become part of the infamous **Nimitz UAP incident**.

"It came out of nowhere," Mitchell told Rockerfeller during their interview at a secluded airstrip in Nevada. "One moment, our radar was clear. The next, this thing was right in front of us. It was moving faster than anything I've ever seen—impossibly fast. And then, just as quickly, it stopped. Dead still, hovering right in front of us."

Mitchell's voice grew tense as he recalled the encounter. "We tried to engage, but every time we got close, it would accelerate away. It was like it was toying with us—like it was aware of our every move. The strangest part? Our instruments were going haywire. Compass, altimeter, radar—everything was out of whack."

Despite their attempts to chase the object, Mitchell and his wingman were never able to lock onto it. The object eventually disappeared, vanishing into the clouds at an impossible speed.

When Mitchell and his crew returned to the carrier, they were immediately debriefed and told not to speak about the incident. Official reports claimed the radar had malfunctioned, but Mitchell knew better.

"It wasn't a glitch," Mitchell said firmly. "We saw it with our own eyes. That thing was out there, and it wasn't ours. The higher-ups didn't want to admit it, but we all knew. We'd encountered something beyond our understanding."

A Remote Village in the Siberian Wilderness

Not all encounters happened in the sky. Some, like the one Rockerfeller learned of from **Viktor Ivanov**, a former Russian soldier, took place in the most remote corners of the Earth. Ivanov had been stationed at an isolated military outpost in the **Siberian wilderness** in the early 2000s when his unit encountered something that defied explanation.

"We were out on patrol, deep in the taiga," Ivanov recalled. "It was the dead of winter—temperatures below freezing, snow everywhere. We weren't expecting to see anything but the occasional wolf or bear. But that night, we saw something much stranger."

Ivanov described how his unit came across a strange, metallic structure in the middle of the forest—a structure that hadn't been there the day before. It was shaped like a dome, with a smooth, silver surface that seemed to pulse with a faint blue light. His unit approached cautiously, but the closer they got, the more their equipment malfunctioned. Radios went dead, compasses spun wildly, and even their rifles jammed.

"It was as if the thing was messing with reality itself," Ivanov said, shaking his head. "We didn't know what to do. We'd never been trained for anything like this."

Before they could get any closer, the dome suddenly lifted off the ground, hovering silently for a moment before shooting off into the night sky, disappearing in a blink of light.

When Ivanov's unit returned to base, they were ordered to remain silent about what they had seen. "The brass told us it was a weather balloon, or some kind of experimental aircraft," Ivanov scoffed. "But we all knew that was a lie. Whatever that thing was, it wasn't Russian—and it wasn't from this Earth."

The Abduction in Arizona

While many encounters involved strange lights or craft, some were far more personal—and far more terrifying. One such story came from **Sarah Jacobs**, a schoolteacher from **Phoenix, Arizona**, who claimed to have been abducted by a UAP while camping in the **Sonoran Desert**.

Jacobs had been camping with friends in the summer of 2020 when they noticed a bright light hovering above their campsite. At first, they thought it was a helicopter or plane, but as it drew closer, they realized it was something else entirely. The light was too bright, and it made no sound as it hovered above them.

"It was like time stopped," Jacobs recalled, her voice trembling as she spoke to Rockerfeller. "I couldn't move. I couldn't scream. I just stood there, staring up at this light."

The next thing Jacobs remembered was waking up in her tent, hours later, with no memory of what had happened in between. Her friends were equally confused, with several reporting strange dreams and feelings of disorientation.

But the most disturbing part came later, when Jacobs began to experience unexplained health issues. "I started getting these headaches—blinding, painful headaches. And then there were the scars. I found these small scars on my arms, my legs, even the back of my neck. I don't know how they got there."

Doctors were unable to explain the cause of her symptoms, and when Jacobs tried to report her experience to authorities, she was met with skepticism and disbelief. "They treated me like I was crazy," she said, her eyes welling with tears. "But I know what happened. I was taken—by something not human."

The Patterns Emerge

As Rockerfeller compiled these personal accounts, he began to see a pattern. These encounters weren't random—they were targeted, deliberate. UAPs weren't simply flying through the skies undetected. They were **interacting** with the world below, in ways that suggested a purpose, an intelligence behind their movements.

Whether it was military pilots, civilians, or entire villages, those who encountered UAPs often described similar phenomena: electromagnetic interference, impossible flight patterns, missing time, and in some cases, physical marks or health effects. These encounters were happening across the globe, from the dense jungles of South America to the deserts of the American Southwest, and yet, governments continued to deny their existence.

For Rockerfeller, these personal stories were more than just evidence. They were the human element in a much larger, much darker conspiracy. While The Cabal worked to suppress information about UAPs and their technology, ordinary people were being affected—sometimes in terrifying, life-altering ways.

But what was the purpose of these encounters? Were these crafts merely observing humanity, or were they actively experimenting, collecting data? And more importantly, who—or what—was behind them?

As Rockerfeller prepared to release a new wave of reports detailing these personal accounts, he knew that the tide was turning. The world was no longer content to ignore UAPs as mere curiosities or the stuff of science fiction. People were demanding answers. And with every new story, every new witness, the truth was coming closer to the surface.

But the question remained: how long would it take before the people in power, those with the ability to control the narrative, silenced these voices once and for all?

Chapter 10:

A Global Government Conspiracy?

As Mr. Rockerfeller continued his investigation, the personal stories of UAP encounters from around the world began to connect in a more disturbing way. Behind the silence, behind the official denials and dismissals, lay an intricate web of global secrecy. He now had more than just testimonies from civilians and military personnel—he had **evidence** of a deliberate and coordinated effort by governments worldwide to control, suppress, and discredit the truth about UAPs.

The personal encounters had painted a vivid picture of an ongoing, and deeply troubling, series of interactions between humanity and some kind of advanced intelligence. But what haunted Rockerfeller the most was **why** world governments were so desperate to keep these encounters hidden. The answer, he was beginning to realize, lay not just in the fear of public panic but in something far more calculated: **global power dynamics** and **technology control**.

The 1961 UN Meeting: A Hidden Pact?

Through a series of carefully worded emails, encrypted phone calls, and hushed conversations in secluded corners, Rockerfeller managed to secure a meeting with **Victor Marchetti**, a former high-ranking CIA officer. Marchetti had long been a controversial figure, known for his criticism of the intelligence community's handling of UFO data. Now in his late seventies, he had spent decades trying to expose what he believed was a vast international conspiracy.

They met in a dimly lit hotel room in **Berlin**, far from prying eyes. Marchetti, gray-haired and frail, spoke with the quiet intensity of a man who had lived his entire life haunted by the knowledge he carried.

"What most people don't understand," Marchetti began, "is that the UFO cover-up isn't just an American thing. It's global. Always has been."

Rockerfeller leaned in, eager to hear more.

"In 1961, during the height of the Cold War, the **United Nations** convened a secret meeting between the world's superpowers: the U.S., the Soviet Union, the UK, and China. The official story was that it was a meeting to discuss nuclear arms control. But the real topic? **UFOs**—or UAPs, as we call them now."

Marchetti went on to describe how the world's most powerful nations had come together not to share information about UAPs, but to agree on how to **control** it. The fear wasn't just of public panic, but of **what would happen if any one nation gained a technological advantage** from UAPs. The pact, as Marchetti described it, was simple: nations would **cooperate** in suppressing information about UAPs, ensure that no single country could monopolize their technology, and work in secret to reverse-engineer any recovered craft.

"The U.S. and the Soviet Union had been enemies on every front," Marchetti said, "but when it came to UFOs, they were allies. They couldn't afford not to be."

Marchetti's words gave Rockerfeller the first clear glimpse into the terrifying scale of the cover-up. It wasn't just about keeping the public in the dark—it was about maintaining the balance of **global power**. Governments weren't just hiding what they knew about UAPs from their people; they were hiding it from each other.

Project Omega: A Secret Global Initiative

From Marchetti's revelation, Rockerfeller began to dig deeper into the history of UAP-related cooperation between governments. What he uncovered next was perhaps the most shocking piece of the puzzle: **Project Omega**, a global initiative that spanned decades, orchestrated by a secretive international organization that coordinated UAP research across multiple nations.

Project Omega, first established in 1965, was a joint operation between the U.S., Soviet Union, and select European nations. Its primary goal was to recover UAP debris, capture any available technology, and develop **classified military applications** using that technology. But Omega was more than just a research initiative—it was a **policy framework** designed to manage the public perception of UAPs.

According to declassified documents, Project Omega was responsible for shaping the way UAPs were discussed—or more accurately, dismissed—in the media. Using disinformation campaigns, the project deliberately seeded false reports of UFO sightings, mixing legitimate reports with outlandish stories to **discredit** any serious inquiry. It employed journalists, scientists, and even Hollywood producers to shape public opinion and make sure UAPs were relegated to the realm of science fiction.

Rockerfeller managed to secure an interview with **Paul Donovan**, a former intelligence analyst who had worked with the British government's secretive UAP task force in the 1970s. Donovan confirmed the existence of Project Omega and described how it operated across borders.

"It wasn't just about recovering technology," Donovan explained. "It was about **controlling the narrative**. Governments were terrified that if the public learned the truth, they would demand answers. And those answers could lead to questions that would shake the foundations of global power."

Donovan went on to describe how Project Omega had even infiltrated the scientific community. Prominent scientists who dared to take UAPs seriously found their careers derailed, their funding cut off. The project had also orchestrated **fake leaks**—controlled releases of information that made it seem like the truth was being revealed, only to mislead the public further. This strategy ensured that the real facts about UAPs remained hidden, even as the public was led to believe that they were getting closer to the truth.

The Connection Between UAPs and Nuclear Sites

As Rockerfeller followed the trail of Project Omega, he began to notice a disturbing trend: many of the most credible UAP sightings occurred near **nuclear facilities**. From **nuclear missile silos** in the U.S. to **power plants** in Europe and Russia, UAPs seemed to show a particular interest in these high-security, high-stakes locations.

One particularly chilling account came from **Captain David Peterson**, a former U.S. Air Force officer who had been stationed at **Malmstrom Air Force Base** in

Montana in 1967. Malmstrom was home to dozens of nuclear missiles, and on a clear autumn night, Peterson and his team witnessed something they could hardly believe.

"It was around midnight," Peterson recalled during an interview with Rockerfeller. "I was on duty in the control room when our instruments went haywire. All of our missile systems started going offline, one by one. We thought it was a technical malfunction at first, but then we got a call from one of the guards outside the silo. He said there was a strange light hovering above the base—bright, silent, and moving unlike anything we'd ever seen."

Peterson's account was corroborated by other officers who were on duty that night. For nearly twenty minutes, the mysterious object hovered above the missile silos, during which time all nuclear systems were **temporarily disabled**. When the object finally disappeared, the systems came back online without explanation.

The official investigation concluded that the incident was caused by an "electronic malfunction," but Peterson and his fellow officers knew better. "That thing wasn't from here," Peterson said firmly. "And it wasn't friendly."

As Rockerfeller delved into similar cases, it became clear that UAPs had a strange connection to nuclear technology. In many instances, UAPs had been reported near nuclear weapons facilities and power plants, often causing unexplained malfunctions or temporarily disabling control systems. This pattern was seen in **Russia, the U.K., France**, and **China** as well.

Was it possible that UAPs were monitoring humanity's nuclear capabilities? And if so, what did it mean for global security?

Whistleblowers from Russia and China

The conspiracy wasn't limited to the West. Rockerfeller soon found himself in contact with a Russian defector named **Sergei Kozlov**, a former KGB officer who had overseen several UAP investigations during the Soviet era. Kozlov described how the Soviet Union had been just as obsessed with UAPs as the U.S., perhaps even more so. The KGB had established a secret division, code-named **The Blue Curtain**, which was responsible for tracking UAP sightings, recovering debris, and studying potential applications for weapons and defense.

Kozlov confirmed what Rockerfeller had suspected: the Soviet Union had its own version of Project Omega, cooperating with the U.S. behind the scenes even as they competed in the open. "We shared data," Kozlov said. "Reluctantly, of course, but we knew that if the Americans made a breakthrough, we couldn't afford to fall behind. The stakes were too high."

In China, Rockerfeller found a similar story. Through a series of intermediaries, he was able to interview **Liang Shen**, a former military scientist who had worked on China's UAP programs in the 1990s. Shen confirmed that the Chinese government had been actively studying UAPs for decades, often in cooperation with other nations, despite public denials.

"We didn't want the West to know how much we had discovered," Shen said. "But we knew they were hiding things from us, too. The truth is, none of our nations were as advanced as these craft—no one had cracked the code, not completely. But we were all trying."

The Big Picture: Global Power and Control

With each new interview, each new piece of evidence, the scope of the conspiracy became clearer. UAPs weren't just a curiosity or a potential security threat—they were the key to **unimaginable power**. Governments around the world had recognized this early on, and they had banded together to ensure that the public never learned the full extent of what had been discovered.

The implications were staggering. If one nation were to fully unlock the secrets of UAP technology—whether it be propulsion, energy, or even time manipulation—it would have an insurmountable advantage over the rest of the world. Wars could be fought and won in seconds. Energy crises would be a thing of the past. Space travel would no longer be a distant dream but a reality.

And yet, for all their secrecy, it was clear that **no government had full control** of the technology. The UAPs, whatever they were, remained elusive, always just beyond humanity's reach. They appeared, observed, and then disappeared without a trace, leaving behind only more questions.

A Document that Changes Everything

One night, as Rockerfeller sifted through the vast archive of documents he had accumulated, he found something that made his heart race. It was a **classified memorandum** from 1978, sent to high-ranking officials in the U.S. and Soviet governments. The memo described a **joint mission** to investigate a downed UAP in the **Arctic Circle**—a mission that had supposedly yielded **living biological specimens**.

The memo was brief, but its implications were explosive. If true, it suggested that governments had not only recovered UAP technology but had also encountered **extraterrestrial life**—and had been covering it up for decades.

Rockerfeller stared at the document in disbelief. This was the smoking gun he had been looking for. It was no longer just about advanced technology or global power struggles. This was about the very **existence of extraterrestrial intelligence**—and the lengths to which the world's governments had gone to keep it hidden.

With this revelation, Rockerfeller knew that the stakes had just risen dramatically. He wasn't just investigating UAP technology or government secrecy. He was now on the brink of uncovering the most profound secret in human history.

But exposing it would come at a cost—a cost he wasn't sure he was prepared to pay.

Chapter 11:

The Race to Control Space

Mr. Rockerfeller stood in the shadows of his dimly lit apartment, staring at the document in his hands—a memorandum so shocking it had turned his investigation on its head. Governments weren't just hiding the existence of UAPs or their technology. They had possibly encountered **living extraterrestrial beings**, and the implications were staggering. The web of global conspiracy, which he had thought centered on UAP technology, had an even deeper layer: control over space itself. This revelation was the final key that would unlock the terrifying truth about the future of humanity's race to control not only UAP technology but the vast expanse beyond Earth.

This chapter would take Rockerfeller deep into the heart of the most secretive programs on the planet, where world powers weren't just competing for dominance on Earth but for supremacy in **outer space**. Whoever could harness the secrets of UAPs would hold ultimate power, not just over nations but over the future of human civilization itself.

The Militarization of Space: From Earth to Orbit

Rockerfeller had long suspected that governments were interested in UAP technology for military purposes, but he had underestimated the **scale** of the competition. As he dug deeper into the declassified documents and testimonies from whistleblowers, it became clear that UAP technology wasn't just being studied for **earthbound** applications. The real goal was the **weaponization of space**.

For decades, treaties had limited the militarization of space. The **Outer Space Treaty of 1967**, signed by most of the world's leading powers, prohibited the placement of nuclear weapons in space and outlawed the use of the Moon and other celestial bodies for military operations. But Rockerfeller's research revealed that despite these agreements, countries like the United States, Russia, and China had been working on **secret military space programs** since the late 20th century.

A highly classified program, known as **Project Eclipse**, had been launched by the United States in 1995. It was designed to study the use of UAP technology for **space-based weaponry**. Documents Rockerfeller uncovered indicated that Project Eclipse had successfully developed prototypes of **energy-based weapons**—weapons capable of targeting satellites, spacecraft, and even objects on Earth. These energy weapons, which were rumored to be based on reverse-engineered UAP systems, could strike with pinpoint precision from space, rendering traditional defense systems obsolete.

Meanwhile, Russia's **Project Lunokhod** and China's **Sky Dragon Initiative** had been conducting their own secret experiments, each with the goal of deploying advanced weapons and surveillance systems in space. These programs were shrouded in secrecy, but according to whistleblowers, both countries had been working to develop **anti-satellite weapons** and **spacecraft capable of neutralizing enemy satellites**—all in the name of gaining strategic dominance in low Earth orbit.

As Rockerfeller pieced together the information, it became clear: **the new Cold War was being fought in space**. But this time, the stakes were higher than ever. Whoever controlled the high ground of space would have the ability to dominate the planet below, not just militarily but economically and technologically.

Private Corporations and the Space Race

While governments were racing to militarize space using UAP technology, they weren't the only players in the game. In the last two decades, private companies had begun to outpace even the most powerful nations in the quest for space dominance. What had once been the exclusive domain of NASA and Roscosmos was now a battleground for private corporations like **SpaceX**, **Blue Origin**, and **Virgin Galactic**.

What most of the public didn't know, however, was that these companies weren't just developing rockets and spacecraft for exploration and commercial space travel. According to the documents Rockerfeller uncovered, many of these companies had **contracts with government agencies** to help develop **military space technologies**—technologies based on UAP research.

One document in particular caught Rockerfeller's attention: a 2018 contract between **SpaceX** and the **Department of Defense**. The contract referenced the development of **quantum propulsion systems**, a technology that sounded eerily similar to what whistleblowers had described as the **anti-gravity propulsion** used by UAPs. If SpaceX had cracked the code on UAP propulsion, it would not only revolutionize space travel but also give the United States a military advantage unlike anything the world had ever seen.

Rockerfeller managed to secure a confidential interview with a former engineer at SpaceX, who confirmed that the company had been working on **classified projects** related to propulsion systems and space-based weapons. "We were playing with technology that felt like science fiction," the engineer said. "Quantum propulsion, field manipulation—it was the kind of stuff you read about in books. But it was real. And the implications? They were massive."

The engineer went on to explain that the race for space dominance wasn't just about exploring the stars—it was about **controlling the next frontier**. "Whoever controls space controls everything," he said. "Commerce, communications, transportation. The future is up there, not down here."

The Race for UAP Technology and Space-Based Energy

Beyond military applications, the pursuit of UAP technology was driven by another, even more transformative goal: **energy**. The concept of **zero-point energy**, which had fascinated scientists for decades, was no longer theoretical. Rockerfeller had uncovered evidence that several governments and corporations were actively researching the possibility of using UAP technology to develop **space-based energy systems**—energy that could be harvested directly from the quantum vacuum of space.

If successful, these systems would provide **unlimited, clean energy**—energy that could power entire cities or even countries. But it would also give whoever controlled that technology a **monopoly on global energy**. Gone would be the days of reliance on fossil fuels, oil, and natural gas. In their place would be **quantum generators** capable of supplying power indefinitely, without any environmental impact.

A document leaked to Rockerfeller from a European space consortium outlined a secret project known as **SkyCore**, a joint initiative between the European Space Agency (ESA) and several private companies. The project aimed to build a **space-based energy station** capable of harnessing zero-point energy and beaming it back to Earth via **microwaves**. The station, according to the document, would be operational by 2035, making Europe the first region to break free of its reliance on Earth-based energy sources.

But the race for space-based energy wasn't limited to Europe. China had already announced its own plans for a **space-based solar power station**, and the U.S. was rumored to be working on a similar project under the codename **Helios**. If these systems became operational, it would mark the beginning of a new era in human history—an era where energy was not just a resource but a **weapon of global control**.

Weaponizing Space: UAP Technology and Space Warfare

While the pursuit of space-based energy had the potential to transform civilization, the darker reality was that much of the research into UAP technology was focused on **weaponization**. The militarization of space was no longer theoretical—it was happening in real time, with governments and corporations working in tandem to create a **space-based arms race**.

The most alarming aspect of this race was the development of **directed energy weapons**—weapons that used UAP technology to create **focused beams of energy** capable of destroying targets from orbit. These weapons, which had once been the stuff of science fiction, were now in the testing phases, according to leaked military documents.

In the U.S., **DARPA** had been working on a secret project known as **Orion's Hammer**, a space-based energy weapon capable of targeting satellites, aircraft, and even ground-based installations from low Earth orbit. Using what appeared to be **plasma-based technology**, Orion's Hammer could deliver a devastating strike with pinpoint accuracy, leaving no physical trace of its origin. Russia and China were rumored to have their own versions of these weapons, though the details were less clear.

One whistleblower from a U.S. defense contractor provided Rockerfeller with chilling details of a recent test of the Orion's Hammer system. "We watched it take out a decommissioned satellite in seconds," the whistleblower revealed. "It was like watching a bolt of lightning—silent, fast, and terrifyingly precise. If these systems go live, it will change warfare forever."

But the most disturbing revelation came from a former high-ranking U.N. official who had worked on arms control treaties in the early 2000s. The official revealed that several nations had secretly **opted out** of key provisions of the Outer Space Treaty, giving them the legal leeway to develop space-based weapons without violating international law.

"We're on the verge of a new arms race," the official warned. "But this one won't be fought on Earth. It will be fought in orbit, in space, and it could determine the future of humanity."

Who Controls Space Controls Earth

As Rockerfeller sat down to review the mountain of evidence he had gathered, the conclusion was undeniable: the race to control UAP technology wasn't just about unlocking the secrets of advanced propulsion or energy systems. It was about **controlling space**—the new frontier of warfare, energy, and commerce. Whoever mastered these technologies would hold the future of humanity in their hands.

But with this power came enormous risk. The weaponization of space could trigger conflicts on a scale never before imagined, with nations vying for control of orbital weapons systems and space-based energy sources. And with UAP technology at the center of it all, the consequences could be catastrophic.

Chapter 12:

The Future of Humanity and UAPs

As Mr. Rockerfeller delved deeper into the global race for UAP technology and the space-based arms race, one question loomed larger than ever: **What does the future hold for humanity if these technologies come into full use?** Could they lead to a new golden age of progress, with limitless energy, interstellar travel, and breakthroughs in science and medicine? Or would they become the catalysts for a new kind of warfare—one where the very fabric of reality could be weaponized, plunging the world into chaos?

These questions led Rockerfeller to seek answers not from governments, corporations, or whistleblowers but from **philosophers, ethicists, and futurists**—people who had been thinking about the implications of UAPs from a human, moral, and existential perspective.

The stakes were clear: humanity stood on the verge of either **unprecedented advancement** or **unimaginable disaster**.

A Turning Point for Civilization

Rockerfeller's first stop was **Professor Linda Dawkins**, a renowned philosopher of science at **Oxford University**. Dawkins had written extensively on the ethical implications of technological advancement, and she had recently turned her attention to UAPs and the impact they could have on global society.

Over tea in her quiet office at Oxford, Dawkins spoke candidly about the potential consequences of humanity's contact with UAP technology. "We're at a pivotal moment in human history," she began, her voice calm but filled with urgency. "If these technologies are truly what they appear to be—quantum propulsion, zero-point energy, dimensional travel—then we're standing at the edge of a revolution unlike anything we've ever seen. But revolutions, as history teaches us, are always dangerous."

Dawkins explained that while UAP technology had the potential to transform humanity's understanding of the universe, it also carried enormous risks. "We're talking about technologies that could collapse the global economy, destabilize governments, and even challenge the foundations of human identity. What happens when you can no longer trust your own senses, when time and space themselves become malleable? What does it mean to be human in a world where the rules of nature no longer apply?"

Dawkins' concerns extended beyond the practical applications of UAP technology. She worried about the **moral consequences** of humanity's pursuit of these advanced capabilities. "We've never been good at wielding power responsibly," she said with a sigh. "Throughout history, every time we've made a major technological leap—whether it was the discovery of nuclear energy or the rise of the internet—our first instinct has been to weaponize it. Why should we expect this to be any different?"

Her words echoed in Rockerfeller's mind as he considered the darker side of the global race for UAP technology. If governments and corporations were already vying for control of space, energy, and military dominance, what hope was there that this technology would be used for the greater good?

The Religious and Existential Implications

In addition to speaking with philosophers, Rockerfeller also sought out **Dr. Ahmed Mustafa**, a renowned theologian and scholar of comparative religion. Mustafa had long been interested in how the discovery of extraterrestrial life—and the technology associated with it—would affect the world's major religions.

They met in a small café in **Cairo**, where Mustafa had spent years studying the intersection of science and religion. Over the clatter of dishes and the hum of conversation, Mustafa explained that the existence of UAPs and their advanced technology could lead to a **spiritual crisis** for many.

"Every major religion on Earth is rooted in the idea that humanity is unique, special," Mustafa said, his eyes thoughtful as he sipped his tea. "Whether you're talking about Christianity, Islam, Judaism, or even certain strands of Hinduism, there's a belief that humanity holds a special place in the cosmos. But what happens when we're confronted with evidence that we're not alone? That there are beings out there—beings more advanced than us?"

Mustafa went on to explain that while some religious scholars had tried to incorporate the possibility of extraterrestrial life into their belief systems, others viewed it as a direct challenge to their faith. "If these beings are more advanced than us, does that mean they're closer to God? Or that they've already surpassed the need for God? These are questions that will shake the foundations of many people's belief systems."

But Mustafa's concerns weren't limited to theology. He also worried about the **existential crisis** that could follow the full disclosure of UAPs. "We've always defined ourselves by our limitations—by the fact that we're bound by the laws of physics, by time, by mortality. If those boundaries start to fall away, if we're no longer the masters of our own fate, what happens to our sense of self? Our purpose?"

Rockerfeller left the meeting with Mustafa realizing that the implications of UAPs weren't just political or technological—they were **deeply human**. The very fabric of society, culture, and identity was at risk of unraveling in the face of this new reality.

The New Space Economy

While the philosophical and spiritual implications of UAPs were daunting, Rockerfeller also turned his attention to the practical effects that these technologies would have on the **global economy**. With the possibility of zero-point energy, advanced propulsion systems, and space-based mining and manufacturing, the very foundation of Earth's economy was on the verge of being overturned.

Rockerfeller arranged a meeting with **Elon Hargrave**, a futurist and economist who had spent years studying the rise of the **new space economy**. Hargrave, a wiry man with a restless energy, met Rockerfeller in his office overlooking **Silicon Valley**, where he explained how UAP technology could both **save and destroy** the global economy.

"We're already seeing it," Hargrave said, gesturing to a holographic map of Earth with space stations, lunar bases, and asteroid mining operations plotted across it. "The new space race is well underway, and it's going to change everything. Once we start mining asteroids, once we have space-based energy systems, Earth's economy will shift in ways we can't even predict yet."

Hargrave explained that the advent of UAP technology could eliminate scarcity—a concept that had driven human economics for centuries. "Zero-point energy, for example, means the end of the fossil fuel industry. Space mining means an end to resource scarcity. But what happens to the global economy when everything that used to be valuable—oil, gas, minerals—becomes worthless?"

The question hung in the air.

Rockerfeller could see both the potential and the danger. If UAP technology became widespread, it could lead to an era of unimaginable abundance. But it could also lead to economic collapse, mass unemployment, and the **breakdown of traditional power structures**. Nations that had built their wealth on natural resources could be rendered irrelevant overnight, while those who controlled space would dominate.

"We're at the edge of a post-scarcity society," Hargrave said, "but that doesn't mean everyone will benefit equally. The corporations and governments who control this technology will have unprecedented power. And if we're not careful, we could see a new kind of feudalism—one where the rich live in space, and the rest of us are left down here on a dying planet."

The Ethical Dilemmas of Disclosure

As Rockerfeller gathered more insights, he realized that one of the most pressing questions facing humanity wasn't just **how** to use UAP technology but **whether** to disclose the full truth. Governments had spent decades keeping these technologies and encounters hidden from the public. Would revealing everything help humanity prepare for the future, or would it lead to panic, chaos, and the breakdown of society?

Rockerfeller reached out to **Dr. Jennifer Nolan**, a political scientist who had worked with several governments on **crisis management and public communication** strategies. Nolan had spent years studying how governments reveal—or conceal—information about existential threats, from nuclear disasters to pandemics.

"We have to ask ourselves: what's the greater good?" Nolan said during their meeting in a quiet Washington, D.C., office. "Full disclosure might feel like the right thing to do—people have a right to know what's happening. But there are real risks involved. Panic, economic instability, the rise of conspiracy movements. If the truth about UAPs is revealed too quickly, without the right context, we could see mass unrest."

Nolan's words were a sobering reminder that the truth, while powerful, could also be dangerous. Rockerfeller had spent years uncovering the secrets of UAPs, but now he faced a moral dilemma: Was humanity ready to learn the full extent of the truth? And if not, how could he release the information in a way that would **help** rather than **harm**?

A Decision That Could Change the World

As Rockerfeller returned to his apartment, his mind raced with the enormity of the decision before him. He had gathered an overwhelming amount of evidence: governments' covert cooperation on UAP suppression, the weaponization of space, the scientific breakthroughs that could end humanity's reliance on fossil fuels. And now, he understood the ethical, philosophical, and economic dilemmas that came with these technologies.

If he released everything, the world would change overnight. There was no telling how people would react. But if he continued to keep the secrets hidden, he would be complicit in the very conspiracy he had spent years fighting against.

The world was on the verge of a new era—one that could either unite humanity in its quest for the stars or tear it apart.

And now, the choice was his.

Chapter 13:

The Unseen Forces Behind UAPs

The decision weighed heavily on Mr. Rockerfeller's mind. He knew that revealing the full truth about UAPs and the government conspiracy could reshape the world—but it could also plunge humanity into chaos. As he mulled over the risks and benefits, he realized that one crucial question remained unanswered: **What is truly behind these UAPs?**

Were they man-made, advanced military technologies? Or were they extraterrestrial in origin, as many believed? Even after all his research and interviews, Rockerfeller still didn't have a clear answer. The testimonies and data he had gathered pointed in many different directions, but none provided a definitive explanation.

One thing was certain: whoever or whatever was behind these phenomena was **watching**—and their motivations remained unknown.

A Meeting in the Desert: Closer to the Truth

As Rockerfeller prepared to take his investigation public, he received an unexpected message. It was from an anonymous source claiming to have information that would "reveal the true nature of UAPs." The sender offered no details but requested a face-to-face meeting in the **Nevada desert**, just outside the infamous **Area 51**.

It was risky, but Rockerfeller felt he had no choice. If this source had information that could definitively explain UAPs, it would change everything. Armed with encrypted communication devices and under the cover of darkness, Rockerfeller made the journey into the desert, following the coordinates provided in the message.

As he arrived at the remote location, the wind whistled across the barren landscape. A lone figure stood in the distance, dressed in black, their face obscured by a hood. Rockerfeller approached cautiously, his heart pounding. The figure remained motionless until he was just a few feet away.

"You came," the figure said, their voice calm and almost mechanical.

"Who are you?" Rockerfeller asked, feeling the weight of the moment. "And what do you know about the UAPs?"

The figure pulled down their hood, revealing a man in his forties, his face lined with stress and weariness. "I'm nobody," he said quietly. "But I worked for the people who are."

He handed Rockerfeller a small metal case. Inside was a **USB drive** and a **document** stamped with a seal Rockerfeller had never seen before—an intricate design that resembled a fusion of military insignia and scientific symbols.

"This contains everything," the man continued. "But once you see it, there's no going back."

Before Rockerfeller could ask any more questions, the man turned and disappeared into the darkness. Alone in the desert, Rockerfeller held the USB drive in his hands, feeling the weight of the information it contained.

The Revelation: A New Reality

Back in the safety of his apartment, Rockerfeller plugged the USB drive into his computer, his fingers trembling. Files immediately began to load—a series of videos, documents, and schematics, each more unsettling than the last. As he opened the first file, his screen filled with grainy footage from the 1970s, showing a team of scientists in what appeared to be a **military laboratory**. The video showed **fragments of UAP debris**, but what shocked Rockerfeller was the presence of **biological specimens—entities** lying on cold steel slabs, their forms vaguely humanoid but unlike anything he had ever seen before.

The document accompanying the video was labeled **Project Elysium**, and it detailed the findings of a secret U.S.-Soviet joint mission to recover a UAP that had crashed in the **Arctic Circle** in 1971. The craft had contained not only advanced technology but **two living beings**. The document described the beings in clinical terms, noting their physical characteristics—large, black eyes, elongated limbs, and a body composition that seemed to **defy biological norms**.

But the most unsettling part was the conclusion. The beings had not survived for long after their recovery, but their physiology suggested they had been able to **manipulate time and space** in ways that the scientists could barely comprehend.

As Rockerfeller continued to scroll through the files, more footage appeared—documents from **China, Russia**, and **the U.K.**, all referencing similar encounters. It wasn't just the U.S. government that had encountered these entities; it was a global phenomenon. And yet, every nation had chosen to **hide the truth**, fearing that revealing these beings' existence would unravel society.

The drive contained a **final message**, written in the form of a confidential memo between global leaders: "The beings are neither gods nor invaders. They are **observers**—and they have been here for longer than we can imagine. Their purpose remains unclear, but one thing is certain: they are waiting."

Interdimensional Beings or Time Travelers?

The more Rockerfeller read, the more the pieces began to fall into place. These beings—whether they were extraterrestrial or something else entirely—were far beyond human understanding. The documents contained references to **interdimensional travel**, suggesting that these beings might not come from a distant planet but rather from a **parallel reality**, one that coexisted with ours but operated under different physical laws.

There were also references to time manipulation—suggestions that these beings might have the ability to move through time as easily as humans moved through space. One scientist had written a chilling note in the margin of a document: **"Are they future versions of us? Are they here to correct our mistakes?"**

The implications were staggering. Could the UAPs be **time travelers**—not aliens but descendants of humanity, returning from a distant future where technological advancements had reshaped biology and physics? Or were they

interdimensional travelers, slipping between realities, observing our world as part of some grand experiment or study?

The documents offered no clear answers, only more questions. But one thing was clear: these beings were not invaders in the traditional sense. They had been **watching**—and manipulating events from behind the scenes—for centuries.

The Cabal's True Role

As Rockerfeller continued to piece together the information, he realized that The Cabal's role in this global conspiracy went deeper than he had imagined. The Cabal was not simply suppressing UAP technology to maintain global power. They were also working to **control humanity's interactions with these beings**—to **manipulate the narrative** and ensure that any contact between humans and these entities was done under their strict oversight.

The final files on the USB drive revealed that **The Cabal** had been in **contact** with these beings for decades. There had been secret meetings, coordinated through intermediaries, where information had been exchanged. The Cabal had learned that these beings weren't interested in conquest or invasion, but rather in **observation** and **control**. They allowed humanity to experiment with their technology—but only to a point.

The Cabal's primary mission was to ensure that no government, no corporation, and no individual ever gained full control over UAP technology. They feared that if humans learned too much, too quickly, they would use it to **destroy themselves**. And so, they created a system of **checks and balances**, allowing limited technological progress but keeping the full extent of UAP knowledge hidden.

This explained why The Cabal had worked so hard to suppress the truth about UAPs. It wasn't just about power—it was about **maintaining balance** in a world that was on the brink of unlocking knowledge that could **alter the course of history**.

The Implications for Humanity

Rockerfeller sat back in his chair, overwhelmed by the weight of what he had learned. The world was not what it seemed. For decades, governments and corporations had fought for control of UAP technology, all while being **watched** by entities from beyond our understanding. The question now was: **What would humanity do with this knowledge?**

If Rockerfeller released this information, it could spark a global awakening—but it could also lead to mass panic. People would have to confront the reality that we are not alone, that there are forces beyond our comprehension manipulating the very fabric of reality.

The choice was no longer just about **exposing** the truth—it was about **guiding** humanity through a revelation that could either unite us in our quest for understanding or tear us apart in fear.

A Final Warning

As Rockerfeller prepared to release the information to the public, his phone buzzed with a message. It was from an unknown number, but the message was chilling:

"You now know everything. But be warned—once the truth is out, you will no longer be protected. Choose wisely."

The message was a stark reminder that he was still being watched—by The Cabal, by governments, and perhaps by the very beings who had been observing humanity for centuries. The future hung in the balance, and Rockerfeller knew that whatever choice he made next would shape the fate of the world.

Chapter 14:

The Choice

The decision that now lay before Mr. Rockerfeller was monumental. The weight of the truth he had uncovered pressed down on him, suffocating him in his small apartment, where the world outside continued to spin in blissful ignorance. He had the power to change everything, to pull back the curtain on a global conspiracy that spanned nations, corporations, and even dimensions. Yet, with that power came the terrifying possibility of chaos.

The message from the unknown number still blinked on his phone screen: **"You now know everything. But be warned—once the truth is out, you will no longer be protected. Choose wisely."**

Rockerfeller understood the implications. Once he exposed the truth about UAPs, he would be a target. The governments of the world, The Cabal, and perhaps even the mysterious beings themselves would come for him. But even more than the danger to himself, he feared what the truth would do to society. Would the knowledge of extraterrestrial or interdimensional life, and the advanced technology hidden from the public, lead to a new age of enlightenment? Or would it plunge the world into chaos, fear, and destruction?

A Plan for Disclosure

Rockerfeller knew that dumping all the information at once—videos, documents, and testimony—would be overwhelming for the public. If he wasn't careful, people might dismiss it as another conspiracy theory or, worse, spiral into fear-driven hysteria. He needed a **strategy**, a way to release the information in stages, carefully controlling the narrative to give humanity time to adjust to the truth.

He thought back to his interviews with whistleblowers, scientists, and ethicists. Nearly everyone had expressed the same concern: the world was **not ready** for the full truth. If the existence of advanced UAP technology and possibly extraterrestrial beings was revealed too quickly, it could destabilize economies, religions, and governments. But the longer the truth was suppressed, the more dangerous it became. Governments were already on the brink of weaponizing UAP technology, and The Cabal had made it clear they would stop at nothing to maintain control.

The world deserved to know the truth—but how much, and how fast?

Rockerfeller began crafting a plan. He would release key pieces of information in carefully timed waves, working with independent journalists, alternative media outlets, and online communities that had already started asking questions about UAPs. He would start with the less explosive revelations—government cover-ups, technological breakthroughs, and testimonies from credible sources—before slowly building up to the more profound truths about interdimensional beings and The Cabal's interactions with them.

It wouldn't be easy. Once the first wave of information was out, there would be no going back. The world's governments and The Cabal would know exactly where the leaks were coming from, and they would mobilize to stop him. But Rockerfeller believed that if he could get enough of the truth out, fast enough, the public outcry would protect him—at least for a while.

The Cabal's Response

As Rockerfeller put the final touches on his plan, another message appeared on his phone, this time more threatening than the last.

"We see you. You've gone too far. This is your final warning."

The message wasn't signed, but Rockerfeller didn't need to guess who had sent it. The Cabal had been watching him for months, and they had already demonstrated their ability to make people disappear. Mark Young had vanished after the release of **The Silent Sky** podcast, and countless whistleblowers and scientists had been silenced over the years. Rockerfeller knew that he was on borrowed time.

But he also knew that The Cabal wouldn't act until he made his next move. As long as the information stayed locked in his encrypted files, they could afford to wait, monitor him, and threaten him into submission. It was only once he **released** the information that they would strike.

With each passing day, Rockerfeller's paranoia grew. He spotted black SUVs parked near his apartment, noticed that his phone calls were being dropped, and sensed the eyes of unseen watchers on him whenever he left his building. He had known the risks when he started this investigation, but now the danger felt palpable, closing in around him like a tightening noose.

There was no time to waste.

Reaching Out to Allies

Rockerfeller realized that he couldn't do this alone. He needed allies—people who believed in the cause and who could help him get the truth out to the world. He reached out to the few journalists he could still trust, including **Lisa Monroe**, who had initially helped him with his research but had grown distant after The Silent Sky podcast went viral. Monroe was cautious, wary of how much deeper she wanted to go into the world of UAPs and government conspiracies, but when Rockerfeller shared the latest files with her, she was hooked.

"This is... beyond anything I ever imagined," she said over the phone, her voice trembling with a mix of excitement and fear. "We need to be careful, though. Once this hits the public, they'll come for us. All of us."

Together, they formed a small but dedicated team of independent journalists, cybersecurity experts, and whistleblowers, all working together to prepare for the information drop. They knew they couldn't rely on mainstream media—The Cabal's reach extended into every corner of the traditional news world. Instead, they would use encrypted communication channels, secure websites, and a network of activists and truth-seekers who had long suspected that something far bigger was being hidden from the public.

Rockerfeller also reached out to **Dr. Evelyn Strauss**, the physicist who had worked on classified UAP research. Strauss had seen too much to walk away now, and she agreed to go public with her findings—on the condition that her safety be guaranteed. She would be the face of the scientific community's involvement, lending credibility to the revelations.

The First Wave: Government Cover-Ups and Technological Breakthroughs

The first release was scheduled for the end of the month. It would focus on the **global cover-up** of UAP encounters, particularly the collaboration between the U.S., Soviet Union, and China. The files included declassified documents from Project Omega, videos of UAP sightings near nuclear facilities, and testimonies from military personnel who had been forced into silence.

Dr. Strauss would lead the scientific disclosures, revealing the technological breakthroughs that had been made using UAP materials. This would include detailed schematics of propulsion systems, zero-point energy theories, and evidence of **anti-gravity technology** being developed by major governments and corporations. These revelations were expected to send shockwaves through the scientific community.

The goal of the first wave was to provide enough **credible evidence** to force the mainstream media to take notice, without overwhelming the public. Rockerfeller's team believed that once the media was forced to cover the story, public interest would grow, and the calls for further transparency would become impossible to ignore.

The Second Wave: Interdimensional Beings and The Cabal

The second wave would be far more dangerous. Once the public had absorbed the revelations about UAP technology and government cover-ups, Rockerfeller planned to release the **interdimensional being** files—along with evidence of The Cabal's interactions with these entities.

This wave would expose **Project Elysium**, the secret joint mission to recover the crashed UAP in the Arctic, and the biological specimens that had been recovered. It would also reveal The Cabal's ongoing efforts to **manipulate global**

events to ensure that no government or corporation gained full control of UAP technology.

The second wave would come with a massive risk. The public's reaction could go in two very different directions: one of **wonder and curiosity**, as people grappled with the idea of otherworldly beings, or one of **panic and fear**, as they realized that humanity had never been in control. Either way, The Cabal would react swiftly, and Rockerfeller knew his time would be limited.

A World on the Brink

With the first wave of information ready to launch, Rockerfeller found himself standing on the edge of history. His entire life's work had led him to this moment. He had uncovered secrets that had been buried for decades, secrets that could reshape the future of humanity. The world was on the brink of an awakening, but with that awakening came incredible uncertainty.

He stared at the screen in front of him, his hand hovering over the keyboard, ready to send the files out into the world. All it would take was one click, and there would be no going back.

The question lingered in his mind: **Was humanity ready for the truth?**

Before he could answer, his phone buzzed again. Another message from the unknown number:

"This is your last chance. Stop now, or face the consequences."

But Rockerfeller had already made his decision. He pressed **send**.

Chapter 15:

The Unseen is Always There

The world was different now. The revelations about UAPs, interdimensional beings, and secret global conspiracies had forever altered the fabric of human understanding. But despite the documents, the testimonies, and the explosive truths that had surfaced, a deep uncertainty still lingered.

As Mr. Rockerfeller sat in the quiet of his apartment, his mind raced. He had seen it all—the technology that defied explanation, the hidden alliances between governments, and the terrifying glimpse into something larger than anyone had ever imagined. Yet, even after everything he had uncovered, **the full truth remained elusive**.

Were UAPs simply the product of human misunderstanding? Were they a manifestation of our own technological and psychological limitations? Or was there truly something **alien**—something far beyond the grasp of human comprehension—lurking behind the veil?

Rockerfeller couldn't shake the feeling that for all the answers he had unearthed, the most important questions still remained. **Who were these beings? What did** they want? And, perhaps most troubling of all: **How long had they been watching us?**

The world had been forced to confront the unknown, but the unknown was vast—endless. The more humanity discovered, the more it became clear how little was truly understood. **The unseen was always there**, lurking just beyond the limits of perception, waiting to be uncovered, but never fully revealed.

Rockerfeller knew that the journey didn't end with the documents he had released. The files, the evidence, and the testimonies were just the beginning. A new age had dawned, one filled with possibilities—and dangers—that humanity had only begun to explore. And even now, as the world adjusted to this new reality, there were still secrets, still shadows, that remained hidden.

A New Message

The night air was cool as Rockerfeller sat at his desk, his computer screen dimmed, his thoughts lost in the quiet. The steady hum of the city outside was a reminder that, for now, life went on. But he knew better than anyone that things were changing.

Just as he was about to close his laptop, a notification appeared in the corner of his screen—an encrypted message, blinking urgently. His heart quickened as he clicked to open it. The sender was anonymous, but the subject line sent a chill down his spine:

"You've only scratched the surface."

The message contained a single attachment. Rockerfeller hesitated for a moment, his finger hovering over the mouse. He knew that opening this file could lead him down a new path—one even more dangerous than the one he had just navigated. But he couldn't help himself. **The truth was out there, and it was calling him again.**

With a deep breath, he clicked on the attachment.

As the file opened, a series of blurry images and classified documents filled his screen. They detailed an incident far more recent than anything he had encountered—an event that had been **completely erased from public record**. The data was unlike anything he had seen before, even more advanced, more chilling. It suggested that not only were UAPs **actively interacting with humanity**, but that something much larger, much more profound, was about to unfold.

Just then, his phone buzzed with a new message—**an unknown number**.

"You're being watched. Be careful, Rockerfeller. This isn't over."

As he stared at the message, a deep sense of foreboding settled in his chest. The story wasn't over. **It had never been over**. The unseen forces were still there, still lurking, still controlling more than anyone could possibly know.

Rockerfeller knew one thing for certain: this was just the beginning of something much, much bigger.

Conclusion:

The Aftermath of Truth

The files were out. In the instant that Mr. Rockerfeller pressed "send," the world began to change. As the information about UAPs, government cover-ups, and interdimensional beings spread across the internet, it was as if a collective gasp echoed across the globe. Thousands of people clicked on the encrypted links, downloading documents, watching videos, and reading testimony from whistleblowers who had stayed silent for decades. Within hours, social media platforms were ablaze with discussions, debates, and speculations.

Some were awestruck, eager to embrace the dawn of a new era of understanding. Others were gripped by fear, unsure of what the revelations meant for the future. Governments scrambled to regain control of the narrative, with hurried press conferences and hastily drafted statements that attempted to downplay the significance of the leaks. But it was too late. The truth was out.

Global Reactions: Wonder and Panic

Around the world, reactions to the information varied widely. In scientific communities, there was a surge of excitement. Physicists, engineers, and researchers who had long speculated about UAPs and advanced technology now had evidence that their theories were grounded in reality. The revelations about **zero-point energy** and **anti-gravity propulsion** ignited new projects, as labs raced to understand and replicate the technology hidden in plain sight.

But the public's reaction was far more divided. For every person who embraced the truth with curiosity and wonder, there were many more who recoiled in disbelief or fear. Religious leaders struggled to make sense of the revelations about interdimensional beings and the possibility that humanity was not alone—or even the most advanced species in the universe. Some faiths adapted quickly, interpreting the UAP beings as part of God's broader creation, while others viewed the revelations as a direct challenge to their foundational beliefs.

In many cities, panic began to spread. Markets plunged as investors reacted to the uncertainty of what these discoveries meant for the global economy. Fossil fuel industries, already in decline, took a massive hit as people realized that **zero-point energy** could render traditional energy sources obsolete. Protests erupted, with some calling for full transparency from governments, demanding that they reveal everything they knew about UAPs. Others, gripped by conspiracy theories, accused world leaders of colluding with extraterrestrial forces to suppress humanity.

But amid the chaos, something else was happening: **hope**.

In scientific circles, there was talk of a new golden age. The potential of UAP technology to revolutionize space travel, energy, and even medicine could open doors that had previously been unthinkable. Humanity stood on the edge of a future filled with promise—if it could navigate the immediate storm.

The Cabal Strikes Back

But Rockerfeller had known from the beginning that his actions would not go unanswered. The Cabal, whose shadowy influence had been exposed, responded swiftly and brutally. Within days of the first wave of revelations, several of Rockerfeller's contacts went dark. Lisa Monroe's apartment was raided, her computer systems wiped clean. Dr. Evelyn Strauss was placed under government protection, though rumors spread that she had been silenced, forced into hiding.

Rockerfeller himself became the prime target. His encrypted communication lines were breached, and agents began tailing him wherever he went. There were reports of an attempted break-in at his apartment, and his phone was flooded with more anonymous threats.

But it wasn't just governments who wanted him silenced. Private contractors, tech moguls, and energy conglomerates, who stood to lose billions if UAP technology became widespread, were equally invested in stopping the leaks. The Cabal's vast resources were now focused solely on Rockerfeller, and it was only a matter of time before they caught up with him.

Humanity's New Frontier

Despite the personal danger, Rockerfeller remained determined. He had given the world the truth, and no matter what happened to him, the revelations would continue to spread. The second wave of documents, detailing the full extent of The

Cabal's interactions with the **interdimensional beings**, was scheduled to be released a week later. But Rockerfeller wasn't sure if he would live to see it happen.

The last few days were a blur of movement—switching locations, using burner phones, meeting with his remaining allies in secret. He had set up a system to ensure that the final wave of information would be released, even if he disappeared. The truth was now beyond his control, and that was all that mattered.

As the world adjusted to this new reality, Rockerfeller realized something profound: the truth about UAPs wasn't just about the technology or the beings who piloted them. It was about **humanity's place in the universe**. For centuries, humans had believed they were at the center of creation, the masters of their own destiny. But now, they were confronted with a much larger, more complex reality—one where **interdimensional observers** existed, where **space and time** could be manipulated, and where the very nature of life itself was called into question.

In the end, the most important question wasn't whether humanity could handle the truth—it was whether humanity could **rise to meet the challenges** and opportunities that came with it.

A Legacy of Truth

As the final wave of documents was released—evidence of The Cabal's deep involvement in global politics, the suppressed breakthroughs in medicine and energy, and the extent of the UAPs' influence on Earth—Rockerfeller knew his role in the story was ending. The world was awake now. The conversation had begun, and it was no longer possible to suppress what had been revealed.

The Cabal would fight to maintain its control, but the balance of power had shifted. Independent journalists, scientists, and truth-seekers across the globe were now mobilizing, refusing to let the information disappear into the shadows again. The world was heading toward a new frontier—a time when humanity would have to decide what to do with the knowledge it had been given.

For Rockerfeller, his work was complete. The risks he had taken, the sacrifices he had made, had been worth it. He had given humanity the truth, and whatever happened next was up to the world.

As he left his final safe house, slipping into the anonymity of the night, Rockerfeller understood that **the future of humanity was now in its own hands**.

Epilogue: The Dawn of a New Era

In the weeks and months that followed the global release of the UAP files, the world slowly began to change. Governments, forced by public pressure, began to open their archives, releasing documents and holding hearings on the suppressed technology. Scientific breakthroughs accelerated, and for the first time, **collaboration across borders** became a priority in harnessing the potential of UAP technology.

But the revelations also left deep scars. Entire industries were destabilized, and the global economy faced unprecedented challenges. Political leaders struggled to maintain control as new power dynamics emerged, and religious communities sought new ways to reconcile their beliefs with the knowledge that humanity was no longer alone.

Despite the challenges, hope remained. The dawn of a **new era**—one of space exploration, energy abundance, and perhaps even contact with other intelligences—was now on the horizon. Humanity's path was uncertain, but for the first time, it was **free** to shape its own destiny, armed with the knowledge that the universe was far larger, and far stranger, than anyone had ever imagined.

And somewhere in the background, Mr. Rockerfeller's name became synonymous with **truth**—the man who had given humanity the greatest revelation of all time.

The End......For Now

Appendices

Case Files and Reports

To give credibility to the UAP phenomenon, here is a collection of declassified documents, witness testimonies, and visual evidence that have surfaced over the years, supporting the existence of UAPs and their potential impact on humanity.

1. Declassified Government Documents

- **The Pentagon's 2020 UAP Task Force Reports (2020-2021)**: Released as part of the U.S. government's acknowledgment of Unidentified Aerial Phenomena, these reports detail various encounters military personnel had with UAPs. Key examples include the famous "Tic Tac" UAP footage recorded by Navy pilots.
    - **Key Findings**: The objects exhibited flight capabilities that defied conventional physics, with no visible propulsion systems and rapid acceleration.
    - **Source**: U.S. Department of Defense – Released under FOIA.
- **Project Blue Book (1952-1969)**: The U.S. Air Force's investigative project into UFO sightings, many of which remain unexplained. While the project was closed in 1969, over 700 sightings remained unresolved and continue to fuel public and scientific curiosity.
    - **Notable Cases**: The **Lubbock Lights** and the **Washington, D.C. UFO Incident**.

- - Source: National Archives.
- **The Rendlesham Forest Incident (1980)**: Often referred to as Britain's Roswell, this event involved multiple military personnel at a U.S. Air Force base in Suffolk, England, who witnessed unexplained lights and craft in the forest.
  - **Key Evidence**: Testimonies from military officers, radar data, and radiation levels recorded at the site of the encounter.
  - **Source**: The UK Ministry of Defence.

2. Witness Testimonies

- **Commander David Fravor (2004)**: A retired U.S. Navy pilot, Fravor famously recounted his encounter with the "Tic Tac" UAP during a training exercise off the coast of California. His testimony, combined with video evidence captured by his jet's tracking systems, has become one of the most credible UAP sightings.
  - **Key Quote**: "This thing would just zip off the screen and show up 60 miles away in a blink of an eye. It was unlike anything we had ever seen."
  - **Source**: Various interviews and UAP Task Force Reports.
- **Lt. Col. Charles Halt (1980)**: Deputy Base Commander during the Rendlesham Forest Incident, Halt recorded his observations on a tape recorder during the event and later gave public testimony, insisting that the UFO was of non-terrestrial origin.
  - **Key Evidence**: A tape recorded in real-time, detailing the encounter.
  - **Source**: Witness interviews, government records.

3. Photographs and Video Evidence

- **The "Tic Tac" UAP (2004)**: Video footage captured by U.S. Navy pilots showing a UAP moving at incredible speeds and performing maneuvers impossible with known technology.
    - **Key Visual Evidence**: Infrared footage, captured using advanced radar and tracking systems.
    - **Source**: Declassified by the U.S. Department of Defense.
- **Phoenix Lights (1997)**: Thousands of witnesses across Arizona and Nevada reported seeing a massive, V-shaped formation of lights moving silently across the night sky. The incident remains unexplained, despite initial claims that the lights were military flares.
    - **Key Visual Evidence**: Multiple photographs and videos taken by civilians.
    - **Source**: Civilian reports and video evidence.

Resources for Further Reading

For readers who want to dive deeper into the UAP phenomenon, below is a curated list of books, documentaries, and websites that explore the subject from various angles, offering insights into the science, history, and conspiracy theories surrounding UFOs and UAPs.

Books

1. **"The UFO Experience: A Scientific Inquiry" by J. Allen Hynek**
   This book, written by the former scientific advisor to Project Blue Book, offers a rigorous exploration of UFO encounters. Hynek is considered one of the most credible scientific voices in UFO studies.

2. **"UFOs: Generals, Pilots, and Government Officials Go on the Record" by Leslie Kean**
   A comprehensive examination of credible UFO sightings from high-ranking officials and military personnel around the world. Kean's investigative work has helped bring legitimacy to the UAP conversation.
3. **"Anatomy of a Phenomenon" by Jacques Vallée**
   Vallée is one of the most well-known UFO researchers, and in this book, he explores the historical and cultural context of UFO sightings, offering alternative explanations that challenge mainstream thinking.
4. **"The Day After Roswell" by Philip J. Corso**
   This controversial book claims that much of the technological progress made in the 20th century is due to reverse-engineering technology recovered from the infamous Roswell UFO crash.
5. **"The Report on Unidentified Flying Objects" by Edward J. Ruppelt**
   Written by the former head of Project Blue Book, this book provides an insider's look at the official U.S. government investigation into UFO sightings during the 1950s.

Documentaries

1. **"The Phenomenon"** (2020)
   Directed by James Fox, this documentary is one of the most comprehensive films on the UAP topic, featuring interviews with military personnel, politicians, and scientists, as well as newly declassified documents.
2. **"Unacknowledged"** (2017)
   This documentary, directed by Michael Mazzola, examines the evidence for a secret UFO program and presents firsthand accounts from government insiders who claim to have worked on classified UAP-related projects.

3. **"Out of the Blue" (2003)**
Another documentary by James Fox, this one explores significant UFO encounters and features testimonies from credible witnesses, including former military personnel and scientists.
4. **"UFOs: The Best Evidence" (1997)**
A multi-part series that provides in-depth coverage of UFO sightings and encounters, from historical cases to modern-day military reports. It remains one of the more serious investigations into the subject.

Websites

1. **The Black Vault**
A repository of declassified government documents related to UFOs, UAPs, and other classified subjects. The site is run by John Greenewald, who has filed thousands of Freedom of Information Act (FOIA) requests to gather evidence about UAPs.
    - **Website**: theblackvault.com
2. **To The Stars Academy of Arts & Science**
Founded by former Blink-182 member Tom DeLonge, this organization focuses on UAP research and disclosure, with several former U.S. government officials and intelligence officers contributing.
    - **Website**: tothestarsacademy.com
3. **National UFO Reporting Center (NUFORC)**
A central hub for UAP and UFO sightings from around the world. This site collects and catalogs reports submitted by civilians, providing a valuable resource for tracking patterns and trends.
    - **Website**: nuforc.org
4. **Mutual UFO Network (MUFON)**
One of the oldest and largest civilian-run organizations dedicated to

investigating UFO sightings. MUFON offers case studies, research, and an international community of UAP enthusiasts and researchers.
- **Website**: mufon.com

Milton Keynes UK
Ingram Content Group UK Ltd.
UKHW042038031224
452078UK00001B/230